SHATTERED

FROM THE EDGE

BOOK ONE

BY EVIE RILEY

SHATTERED

Can two young gay men survive the hate and find love?

Jimmy Ashford's senior year is looking good. His part-time job hours are lining up perfectly with studying and his future goals. With his parents behind him all the way, he knows he is one of the lucky ones when it comes to support and love. He's gay, out, and proud.

He can't wait to graduate and go off to Art School. Being an artist is all he's ever dreamed about. Well, except now there's the new sexy-as-sin Zane Hamilton. Life is suddenly a lot more interesting, but can Jimmy tolerate being Zane's dirty little secret?

Zane Hamilton only has a few more years before he will be free of his controlling parents and is finally able to start his dream for the future. If only he can make it that long. His father is determined he work in the family business and marry a woman he has zero interest in. If he doesn't comply, his whole future is at risk.

As manager of the quaint little diner in town, he has no business staring at one of the staff, but Jimmy is so free and confident, gorgeous too. Everything he wants. Everything he needs. Keeping his eyes, and hands, off Jimmy is torture, and he hates keeping Jimmy in the background like a dirty little secret, but if his parents find out he's gay all hell will break loose.

Is Zane willing to stand up for Jimmy, for their love?

CHAPTER ONE

Jimmy

THE SOUND OF the final bell going off had never sounded sweeter to me than right this moment. I had a love for school, but that last class in the day, political science, could really drag on for centuries. Some days, like today, it took all of my strength just to physically keep my eyes open.

I quickly got the hell out of there and made my way toward my locker. Being eighteen and a senior in high school came with a good batch of mixed feelings. Sadness, because the school you had spent the past four years in, growing up in, was no longer going to be in your life. All of the teachers and friends you had made along the way weren't going to be sitting next to you at lunch or making you laugh in the library just to upset the world's crankiest librarian. It was a piece of your life that was finished and it was bittersweet because your future was waiting for you right around the corner. For me, my future was waiting for me six blocks from here, at my part-time job.

I hastily said goodbye to the people I knew in the hallway as I made my way out of the building. I had to get to my work so I wouldn't be late. I had made a habit of never being late for work and I was not about to start now.

Working at the diner wasn't fascinating, and it didn't help me with my art, but it paid me every two weeks and that money went toward art supplies and my savings for when I went off to college in the fall. Plus, working at the diner was not that bad. There were certainly worse part-time jobs I could be doing. In a city like Gaithersburg, Maryland you still had that small town feel, even though there was a decent size population, just under sixty thousand. Most would find that small, but when you think about how some cities only have a couple thousand people, I would say Gaithersburg was a decent size.

With that small town feel, though, you still had people with small town beliefs, like religion, politics, and sexual orientation. Two out of the three you could easily hide, but the sexual orientation part was a bit harder. Eventually, someone would notice you holding the hand of someone that was the same gender as you. Don't get me wrong, there were a lot of forward thinking people. A lot of accepting people who didn't care who you loved as long as you were happy. It was those people that got someone like me, a gay teenager, through the harder days.

My parents are some of those people. They are truly amazing. I'd been such a nervous wreck when I'd decided to come out to them when I was fourteen. I'd been terrified with how they would react.

They'd always been supportive of me where my art was concerned, but I also knew it was one thing to accept that your son was never going to be a football player and another that he was gay. They had taken it like a dream.

I was all prepared for a big showdown. I'd practiced what I was going to say to them and I was prepared for any argument they were going to throw my way. All of my hard work was wasted when my mom just simply said they knew and asked what I wanted for dinner. I had gone in fully prepared that my parents were going to be shocked. Only for the tables to be turned, leaving me the one that was stunned stupid in the living room.

All of my stress and worrying had been for nothing, absolutely nothing. I was so shocked and ecstatic that I went to school the very next day and told my friend Danny all about it. He had wanted to tell his parents about being gay, but he was really worried with how religious they were. He finally told them earlier this year. Only it didn't go over so well.

He'd called me that night crying his eyes out because his parents had kicked him out. All he had left was his backpack and a single duffle bag with his clothes and personal belongings. They completely threw him out without even a second thought about where he would go. I had immediately told him to come to my house and my parents both agreed that he could stay with us if he couldn't stay with his older brother who had his own apartment in town.

Thankfully, Danny's brother was not

a jerk and had been pissed at his parents for kicking out his kid brother. Danny moved in with him and never had to hide who he was again. Neither of them have spoken to their parents since that night and I doubted they ever would.

That night, though, gave me a whole new level of respect for Danny. He had shown some true courage to tell his parents and then when they forced him to leave, he didn't try and put the genie back into the bottle. He held his head up high and became a proud gay kid. It was only proof to how strong he was and I couldn't have been more proud of him.

The aroma of the diner welcomed me as I stepped through the door for my shift. Most would find it gross, I suppose, but to me it smelled like the fifties. I can't explain it, but the odor from the grill with the eggs, the sweet sugar smell of waffles, the rich scent of brewed coffee, it always reminded me of poodle skirts and really bad hairstyles.

It didn't look like the fifties, but the Main Street Diner had been here since then. The one wall to the left of the diner was covered in photos from the past eight decades. They weren't organized at all, either, just thrown up where there was a spot. The owner, Anthony Blackstone, had taken over the diner from his father. It had been in their generation since the very first day. They were a pillar in the community and everyone still came here, even with some of the National chain restaurants just down the street. You just couldn't beat the food here, especially for breakfast.

SHATTERED

"Hey, Sal, how are you?" I called to one of my regulars.

He was a very sweet seventy-year-old man who used to come here with his wife. They had been married for forty years before he lost her to cancer two years ago. They used to come here every Thursday night to have date night. They had their first date right here in the diner almost fifty years ago. Every Thursday, they would come in and sit in the same booth every single time. We would make sure no one sat in it before they had the chance to get here.

Sal had been coming here after her death, still. He would sit in the same spot and place her framed photograph across from him. It sounded really sad, I know, but to him it was his way of still having their date night together.

He once told me that there were many days where he missed her so much it hurt, but when he came to the diner for their date night, he felt connected to her. The pain didn't hurt so much and he truly believed that she was sitting in that booth seat right across from him. It was the sweetest thing I had ever heard, still to this day.

I didn't know if I believed in spirits or not, but what I did know is that I hoped it was true. I hoped that Martha was sitting right there in that booth with Sal, spending time together until they could be reunited again.

"I'm still moving, Jim," Sal said, flashing a toothless grin.

"I'm happy to hear that. This place wouldn't be the same without you, Sal."

I made my way toward the back room

so I could drop my coat and bag off. I was hoping it might be a little dead tonight so I could get a jump-start on my homework. Dead was never good for tips, but it did allow me to get my homework done before getting home, allowing me the time to relax and watch a couple episodes of my favorite show before I would have to go to sleep.

After clocking in, I made my way behind the counter and gave Stella a big smile. "Hey good looking, how's it been?" I asked.

In her thirties now, Stella had been working here for ten years. She'd dropped out of high school at sixteen when she got pregnant. Her boyfriend at the time was a high school senior and he took off right after graduation before their daughter was even born. She came from a single mother, who kicked her out once she discovered that she was pregnant. Stella didn't let it get to her, though. She persevered and she created a life for her daughter. She had been working odd jobs for the first four years before she was given the opportunity to work here full-time. Mr. Blackstone was really good with her and even gave her health benefits for her daughter after she had worked here for six months. Stella had been eternally grateful to Mr. Blackstone and as a result, she always came into work and even worked extra shifts if they had no one to cover. She was a hard and loyal worker and I loved her from the first day we met.

"Not too bad, Jimmy. You know how Thursdays are. How was school?"

"It was uneventful, which is exactly

how I like it. I have some homework, but if it's dead in here later I can always work on it."

"You must be getting excited with graduation creeping up," Stella said, flashing a warm smile.

"I guess I am. I don't know, it doesn't feel real yet. Maybe it would be different if I was going to travel the world or move to a completely different State. But to me, it just feels like I'm going to school in the fall. Only this one will be like a boarding school that I get to come home for on weekends," I said with a shrug.

"Don't worry about that too much. It will feel more real once you are living in the dorms. Then, in your second year, you'll be getting your own place. It'll sink in once you're there and taking classes."

That sounded about right. I wasn't

the type of person who got excited to begin with, really. Of course, I was looking forward to it, but I wasn't jumping up and down with excitement.

Before anymore could be said, the little bell above the door chimed and we both looked up, expecting to be greeting a customer. Instead, we saw our new manager walking in.

We had been told a few days ago that we would be getting a new night manager. Stella had been offered the job, but she liked being a server. She liked the lack of responsibility more than anything. She said she had enough going on with raising a teenager; she didn't need more of a headache. She was open to the idea at a later time, though, when her daughter was off to College herself.

SHATTERED

I had been prepared for the new manager to be someone like the old manager, Mr. Wilson, older and not really attractive. This man, though, he was nothing like I was expecting.

He had short brown hair; much like myself only mine was blond. He had a clear five o'clock shadow that he had no interest in trying to get rid of, which was fine by me. I liked a man that looked a bit rough. He was well built, like he spent some time working out at the gym in his day, but he wasn't so muscular that it was the only thing he did in the day. He walked with his head held up high and his back straight.

He didn't appear to be nervous at all for someone starting a new job. He glanced over at us and I felt a quick, warm shot of arousal at seeing his emerald green eyes. It was only for a moment before he was heading into the back, but I could have sworn he had mesmerized me with them. I couldn't take my eyes off of him, even after he had disappeared into the kitchen area. My gaze lingered on the door, hoping he would come back out.

"Earth to Jimmy, come back, you're drooling," Stella teased.

"I don't drool," I said, feeling my cheeks warm as I forced myself to look back over to her.

That granted me a chuckle. "Man, if I knew the new manager was going to look like that, I would have worn tighter pants." Stella winked.

"I think I should have worn looser ones," I joked back. But in all honesty, getting a hard-on at work was not a good idea. Thankfully, I had a server's apron on that would hide any issues should something get out of control. And by something, I mean my imagination. Hey, I was an artist; I had a remarkable imagination.

One that had gotten me through many lonely nights.

"You're so bad. What do you think, straight or gay?"

"You know, most people worry if their new boss is going to be a dick or not. Not what team they play for," I said with a playful smirk as I leaned my left side against the counter. I was not going to admit out loud that I was wondering the exact same thing.

And praying it was the latter.

"I doubt he's a dick. He doesn't look old enough to be a dick. He's like twenty, maybe twenty-one. And I'm allowed to wonder all I want. I'm just not allowed to ask. I'm going with straight, though. He's got that straight boy look."

"Can't argue with that. He's very pretty, though."

He was most likely straight. Odds were in his favor for being straight, but that didn't mean I couldn't window shop to my heart's content.

I didn't have much time to ponder my new boss, because a table of four teenagers walked through the door. I went back to focusing on my work. Whatever was going to happen with our new manager would happen regardless of what I wanted. For now, I would wait until I would get to be introduced.

***

It was a good two hours later when I had

a moment to catch my breath. The dinner rush had come through and it was always busy for a few hours before everyone started to head out for home. Then only a few stragglers would come in for a late dessert or a coffee before they got back on the road. While I was in the middle of filling the napkin dispensers once again, Mr. Wilson made his way out of the kitchen with the new manager.

"Jimmy, meet our new night manager, Zane Hamilton," Mr. Wilson said.

Zane.

The name suited him. Strong, masculine, but unique. It wasn't a name you heard every day in your life. Seeing Zane up close like this only allowed me to realize that he looked even more sexy up close and personal than he did from a distance.

His eyes were to die for. I had never seen eyes this green before. He had a strong jaw and chiseled facial features that gave him a model like look. He was truly breath-stealing to look at up close. This man was a heartbreaker and I had no doubt that he would have a trail of hopeful lovers behind him.

I sighed inwardly, knowing working for this sexy-as-sin man would be a challenge of the worst kind on my active imagination.

"Hi, it's nice to meet you, Sir," I said, trying to remember that this was my boss and I needed to be polite and friendly. I was leaving for College come the fall, but I needed this job to make sure I could have enough saved up until

I found a job up there.

"Call me Zane, please." His voice held a slight gravelly tone to it, but it wasn't from something like smoking. It was completely natural and it sent a shiver right down my spine.

"Well, it's nice to meet you, Zane. I'm sure you will love working here, the customers are great and the other employees are really friendly. If you have any questions, don't be afraid to ask."

God, yes, please ask me anything you want.

I would love to talk with him for my whole shift. Anything that would allow me to get close to him. I bet he smelled amazing.

"Thank you, I appreciate that. I'm sure I will love working here."

I knew *I* was going to love him

working here. This job just got so much better. I couldn't stand around and talk, though, because I had a new table come in and the last thing I wanted to do was leave a bad impression on my new boss.

I sighed, made my excuses, and quickly went back to work, waving goodbye to Mr. Wilson as he headed out. I did my best to focus on my work, but I could feel eyes on me. Zane's eyes. I knew it without even having to look at him.

I didn't have a problem being watched. I mean, it's common when you get a new boss. A good manager would always look around, check out how you work and what habits you had, or even what routine there already was in place. So Zane watching me throughout my shift wasn't that out of the norm.

SHATTERED

The thing was, though, he wasn't looking at me like he was evaluating my skills. He was just following me around with his eyes. It was a little awkward and it left me feeling a bit weirded out by it. That was, until I saw just the slightest glimmer of what could only be described as lust in his eyes when I bent over the table to wipe the far end of it. I looked up just in time for him to snap his eyes away and look over at another customer.

Oh my god!

Is he checking me out?

That couldn't be right, right?

There was no way that he would be checking me out. Even if he was interested in guys, why would he be interested in someone like me? I couldn't be his type. As badly as I wished I was his type. Guys like him wouldn't go for the artistic type like me. I had enough experience in my dating life to know that.

Still, though, the thought of him checking me out didn't leave me feeling awkward or creeped out. It left me feeling a tingle of excitement. I knew nothing could come from it and I was perfectly okay with that.

One thing I did know, work was going to be so much more enjoyable.

CHAPTER TWO

Zane

WALKING INTO A new job on that first day was always daunting, but this time around it was a little bit different. Today, I wouldn't be working some low level position; I was going to be in management. Yes, it was only managing a diner, but I was still responsible for the staff and ensuring that everything went according to plan on my shift. It was not a responsibility I would be taking lightly.

Today was so much more than just another job, though. Today was the first day that I would be getting true hands on experience in the industry I wanted to build a career in. It wasn't a diner I wanted to own, but a resort. Not just any resort, though, the best on the East Coast.

A place where people came from all over the world to visit.

Something that would prove to my father that I was worthy of my name and his respect.

Most people have their parents' respect by just being themselves and doing their best, but not me. My father liked to say that we come from old money and with that came a responsibility and prestige that we needed to upkeep. Anything less than perfection and we were not only letting ourselves down, but every family member that came before us. It was a lot of pressure to be perfect. To get perfect grades all throughout school. If I came home with anything but A's, I would be grounded and forced to take summer school to better my grade. I could have understood it if it was to ensure I got into an Ivy League school, but my father made it very clear that I was to not go to University. That it wasn't needed and would be a waste of money. I would be working for the family business, learning everything I could so I could take over it one day. Most people would find that comforting. To know that you would always have a job, but to me it was just one more way my father could control my life.

My whole life had been the same. He didn't care that I wanted to play baseball. He put me in golfing instead. Said it would help me to meet the right type of people that I could network and build connections with for future business deals. I was eight at the time.

My life had been planned out without any say or input from me. When I was younger I should have spoken up more, should have rebelled and done what I wanted, what would have made me happy. At the time, though, I just wanted my parents' love, my father's love. What all little boys wanted.

Now, at twenty-one, I was terrified of my father discovering the truth. That I didn't want to manage a pharmaceutical company. I wanted to build a resort that would go down in history. That would allow me to build an empire that could sustain the test of time. Something that could be passed down to my children, assuming they wanted it.

What I wanted to scream at my father most, though, was that I didn't want to marry whatever woman he picked for me. I wanted to marry the *man* that I would pick for me. I was gay, very much gay, and it was a secret that I would never be able to tell them. You would think with it being the twenty-first century that people wouldn't have to hide their own sexuality. Well, the twenty-first century has yet to meet my parents, specifically my father. If he were to discover that I preferred the company of men over women, he would go absolutely nuclear. I would be shipped off to some conversion camp for the rest of my life if that is what it took to make me see things his way, get over *those* perversions. He would never allow for his son to be gay, for any of his children. Thankfully, my kid brother was straight and he would never have to deal with the pain of having to hide something like this.

Having to hide this part of myself, this huge part, has not been easy. There have been guys I have dated since I discovered that I was gay. I was sixteen at the time and all it took was one look from Shawn Roman, the school's baseball shortstop, and I knew I was different. I wasn't interested in girls, even the ones that obviously flirted with me. But when Shawn walked into Math class, oh yes, I noticed. And he noticed me.

Being with Shawn was easy, he was in the closet just like me and he had zero interest in breaking out of it. He had his eye on a sports scholarship so he could work his way up to the major league. It was perfect for a long time, well, seven months, but back then it felt like years.

Shawn had come to school one day with Daisy on his arm, his new girlfriend that he had no problem making out with in the hallways for everyone to see, myself included. That is when we broke up, a difference of opinions.

To Shawn, it wasn't cheating because she was a girl and he was gay. She didn't turn him on. She was just what he needed so people wouldn't suspect he was gay. She was his beard.

To me, kissing was kissing and it didn't matter if it was a guy or a girl. They were still making out and fooling around. I wasn't going to be sharing him and ultimately he picked her over me. Or I guess I could say, he picked his closet over me.

The thing is, I couldn't really be pissed at him for it, because when I was nineteen I was the one having to pretend that I was straight while seeing Chris. Chris who was out and proud and the most flamboyant gay person I have ever met. He didn't want to be a dirty little secret, not that I could blame him, but I couldn't leave my closet. That was the end of that relationship, and truly the last time I have tried to date anyone.

I've had one-night stands with guys

that I've hooked up with at one of the gay clubs within the nearby towns. Nothing ever serious, though, since Chris. It wouldn't be fair to date someone that would have to live a lie, be a secret, until the day came when I could finally come out to my family. That day wouldn't be until I was twenty-five and able to secure my trust fund. With my trust fund in my own name and my father no longer having control over it, I could open my resort and come out to them. It would mean I could finally just be me and not someone they wanted me to be, someone *he* wanted me to be. It was a day I was counting down to, literally. One thousand, two hundred, and seventy-five days until I was free. As if I was counting down a prison sentence, and in a lot of ways I was in prison. I had been serving a twenty-five year sentence for a crime I didn't commit. My freedom would come though and it was going to be remarkable. At least, I hoped it would be.

"All right, you are all set," Mr. Wilson said with a warm smile.

Today was my first shift, but he seemed pretty confident that I wouldn't screw anything up. Though, with the checklist that I had to follow before I could leave, it would be pretty hard to make a mistake.

"Thank you for all of your help, Mr. Wilson."

"You are doing me a huge favor. Now that you will be working at night, I no longer have to. I get to go back to my nice day shifts and be home at a decent hour. Come on, I'll introduce you to the staff that is here."

Mr. Wilson stood and slowly walked out of the office. The man was old, too old to still be working, in my opinion, but it was a sad fact that retirement was not an easy concept to achieve anymore.

It was one of the things that I wanted to make sure I offered my employees once my resort was successful and profitable. I would make sure they had medical insurance and a pension. If you worked your whole life, you shouldn't have to be penalized because you couldn't work for a company that offered you a pension so you could retire.

We made our way through the small diner and Mr. Wilson introduced me to the night cook, Matt, then he took me to the front where I met two of the servers. First, Stella. She was a bit older than me, but she seemed very friendly and didn't seem to have a problem with having to listen to someone younger than her. Then Mr. Wilson introduced me to quite possibly the most beautiful man I have ever met. Jimmy.

"Jimmy, meet our new night manager, Zane Hamilton."

"Hi, it's nice to meet you, Sir," Jimmy said, and flashed the most beautiful white smile I had ever seen.

"Call me Zane, please," I managed to get out without looking like a complete fool—I hoped.

I couldn't get over how beautiful he was, and his voice... God, it was smooth and rich, like high-end milk chocolate. I could listen to him talk all day and never get tired of it. Hell, he could read the phonebook and he would captivate me.

It shouldn't be possible for a man to be this beautiful. His skin was a smooth porcelain color. It wasn't white in the sense that he never went outside, it was his natural skin tone and he clearly took care of himself. He was cleanly shaven, not even a hint of a five o'clock shadow on his face like I had. His eyes were as blue as the ocean and I could easily get lost within their depth. His hair was a sun kissed, light brown that was kept a bit longer. It wasn't long, but it wasn't short, that nice middle ground like I had.

This was not good. I was supposed to be his manager; someone working for me could not be this attractive. There was no way I was going to be able to keep my eyes off of him. I was already looking forward to him walking away so I could see his ass. I was in so much trouble.

"Well, it's nice to meet you, Zane. I'm sure you will love working here, the customers are great and the other employees are really friendly. If you have any questions, don't be afraid to ask," Jimmy said, a warm smile turning up the corners of his mouth.

There was only one question that mattered to me right now. Well, two.

The first, was he gay?

And the second, if yes, how much trouble would I be in if I pushed him down onto a table and had my way with him?

"Thank you, I appreciate that. I am sure I will love working here."

Jimmy gave me one last smile before he turned to head over to a new table. Sure enough, his ass looked amazing in the black skinny jeans he wore. It took every ounce of strength I had to keep the moan in my head.

I gave Mr. Wilson a warm smile goodbye as he said he was heading out now, leaving me in charge of the diner. When I started, my biggest concern was making sure it was still standing come the end of the night. Now, my biggest concern was making sure I didn't get a sexual harassment lawsuit by the end of the night.

The vibrating of my phone had me moving into the back office. A quick look at it had my heart plummeting into my stomach.

My father.

Most kids call their parents Mom and Dad, but not me. I'd always been raised to refer to them as Mother and Father. It was to show a higher level of respect for their sacrifice and position within the family. That was exactly how my father explained it to me when I was just four years old. At the time, I had no idea how screwed up it was, I figured everyone must call their parents that. It wasn't until I started getting older that I came to discover it was screwed up.

There was always that doubt within me that my parents, especially my father, actually did love me. Love me and my kid brother. They weren't affectionate; they weren't the type of parents that tucked you in at night when you were younger. Even if we were sick, we were pretty much on our own. It's why I've always made a point of being there for Daryl. I didn't want him to have to grow up being stuck in bed sick and miserable knowing that no one was going to be there to help him. I wanted him to know, on some level, at least, what love was supposed to feel like. What it felt like to be hugged and taken care of. I couldn't change my own childhood, but I could have some say and control over the outcome of his. It was one of the reasons why I had been trying so hard to keep my father's attention on me. If he continued looking at me and my future, then Daryl was free to fly under the radar and discover who he was.

Letting out a sigh, I closed the office door and answered my phone. Letting it go to voicemail was never a good idea where my father was concerned.

"Hello, Father."

"Zane, I just received confirmation for

dinner tomorrow. Make sure you are here by six o'clock sharp, and look presentable. This dinner with the Millers is very important for the future."

How could I possibly forget about dinner tomorrow night?

Henry Miller owned a head corporation that boasted fifty hospitals within the country. All of them were privately owned and made millions every year in profits. My father had made friends with him five years ago in an effort to push his pharmaceutical company to the next level. It had worked, but ever since that day the Millers had been a serious pain in my ass. It wasn't Henry, per say, but rather the fact that he had a daughter, Kayla, who was my age. Both of our fathers thought we would make the perfect power couple. A way to merge both of our families together, and potentially, one day, the two companies. Kayla was all for it, which didn't help the situation. Obviously, I was not all for it.

"I know, Father. I will make sure I'm home and ready for when they arrive." I just needed to humor my father and bide my time. Soon enough, I would be in the clear.

"This dinner is very important, Zane. If all goes according to plan, it will cement the future of my company. I want you respectful and paying a great deal of attention to Kayla. Make her feel special and let her know you have a genuine interest in her. Henry has told me she is already interested in you. You just need to seal the deal now."

Leave it to my father to refer to a

relationship as a deal. Though, I suppose in his eyes that is exactly what he saw this as. To him, it didn't matter if I wanted to be with her or not. Hell, he didn't even ask if I thought she was attractive or even had an interest in dating her. He did what he always did. He ordered and controlled without a single thought about how anyone else would feel.

"I will be very respectful, Father. I have to go, though, I'm at work and I need to make sure everything is in order. I want to make a good first impression on my boss."

"You better be making a *great* first impression. The Hamilton name is not one that can be squandered. Even if you are slumming it working in a diner," he said, not even bothering to hide his disdain for my new job.

"I am, Father. I really must be going, though."

In all honesty, I didn't have anything I needed to do. All I could do was wait for closing time and make sure nothing blew up. I just had no desire to keep talking with him. I would much rather stand in the corner and watch Jimmy work all night. It was pathetic, I was aware, but at this point all I could do was window shop when it came to men. If I was going to be stuck window shopping for the next three years, I might as well do it with a man as breathtakingly beautiful as Jimmy.

"Do not be late tomorrow."

That was all my father had to say before he ended the call. What was odd, was how he kept repeating for me to not be late. I still lived at the house, not by my doing but his, so it wasn't like I wouldn't be home at some point within the next twenty-four hours.

Pocketing my phone, I headed back out to the restaurant section of the diner. It was surprisingly busy considering it wasn't quite dinner hour yet. I had never been here before I applied, but I could see that there was a steady flow of regulars. And from what I had seen so far, the food looked and smelled delicious. I couldn't help but wonder what Jimmy smelled like.

Would he have his own scent, or would the scent of the diner be on him?

I was a firm believer that you could tell what type of a man someone was by their scent. Guys who had a woodsy smell to them, tended to be very outdoorsy and good with their hands. Guys who smelled like aftershave and overpowering cologne, tended to be jerks and had no life skills. I would take an outdoor man over a boardroom stiff any day of the week.

Leaning against the entrance between the kitchen and the dinning room allowed me to have the perfect view of Jimmy, without it looking like I was watching him. He moved with grace from one table to the next. The easy smile on his face as he talked with the customers told me he was friendly and kind, but also confident in himself.

He was thinner, so he clearly didn't workout all day or play sports. He wasn't a stick either, though, so he did do some form of working out. My guess was a runner if his thighs were anything to go by. It wasn't just his appearance that had caught my attention. It was how easy he smiled. He seemed so carefree and not weighed down by life and expectations. His parents probably not only loved him, but liked him. He probably had a girlfriend he was madly in love with. He was free. Free to be himself and live his life how he saw it. I wanted that freedom. I wanted to be able to smile with ease just like him.

Four years. Four more long years.

***

Ten minutes, that's how long I had left before the circus would start. Ten minutes left of being able to be myself before I would need to play straight and interested for an entire dinner. I was really not looking forward to this at all, but I also knew I had no choice in the matter. I would just need to get through this and then I could focus on my work and my life.

I headed outside for a quiet moment alone before all the fanfare began but the sight of my kid brother crying quickly interrupted that plan. Daryl was always a tough kid. He didn't cry. He didn't get emotional. He was athletic, but he was also artistic. I knew he hid that side of himself quite often because of our father. Our Father wasn't one for creative outlets. He believed men to be a certain way and a painter was not one of them. Daryl had always done his best to live up to our father's expectations. I knew it was hard on him, though, because he didn't fit into one category. He was a jock that could paint a mural that would leave you speechless. All of the emotions that he had seemed to come out on the canvas. He was different compared to me, in that sense. I kept everything inside. I put up a front and just pushed through the day with a mental clock ticking down the days in my head.

I quickly made my way over to the bench by the pond where he sat. I made a point of not sitting next to him, wanting to give him some space. We were close, but we weren't that close, either. We used to be really close when we were younger, but then I became a teenager and started to hang out with my friends. I didn't want my kid brother hanging around. He started to get busy with being in different sports, plus when he had free time he was always drawing or painting. He was seventeen now and months away from turning eighteen. He was set to graduate this year and I had no idea what he was going to do after high school. I was really going to have to get better with him, do better. I was supposed to be his older brother and I didn't even know what his dreams were. What his plans were for his life.

"What's wrong, Squirt?"

The snort that came from him only caused me to smile. It was a nickname I had for him since he was born. He used to love it, but once he became a teenager he hated it. Still, it was his nickname and I would always call him Squirt.

"Nothing," Daryl said as he wiped at his eyes to try and stop the tears from flowing.

"I can count on one hand how many

times you've cried since you were twelve. You don't care for nothing. Hell, you didn't cry when you broke your arm. Something is going on, what is it?"

"Like you care."

That cut deep, but he had a valid point. I had been a pretty shitty brother in the past few years. "I know I haven't been around much. Me not being here, though, that much isn't because of you. It's just Father, I don't want to be around him. So it's easier for me to be working or out all night so I don't have to deal with him. That doesn't mean I don't love you or care about you. Something is going on with you. Tell me. I might be able to help."

I was really hoping he would open up to me. Clearly something was bothering him and he shouldn't have to feel like he had to face this world alone. Daryl sniffed a few times before he cleared his throat and spoke.

"I was dating someone for the past year now almost. I just found out they had been cheating on me for half of that time. Then I was the one dumped so they could be with someone else."

Okay, not what I expected. I had no idea he was even dating someone.

How could I have missed something this important in his life?

For a year he had been dating a girl and I never even met her. At seventeen, a year was pretty serious.

"I know it hurts, but if she is dumb enough to cheat on you, then she's a loser and you deserve someone so much better. I know it hurts and it will for a little bit, but you will find another girl and she will make you forget all about your ex. She doesn't deserve your tears."

"He," Daryl said softly.

"He who?"

"I wasn't dating a girl. I was dating Brad. I'm gay, Z," Daryl admitted as he looked at me out of the corner of his eye.

He was waiting to see how I would react. He knew just as much as I did how our parents felt about homosexuality. It would be logical that he would be worried about what I thought about it. I was shocked, though. I had no idea he was gay.

We are both gay.

It was this moment, though, that I realized something about my brother that I had never realized before. He was braver than I was, because he actually said it out loud. While I had been trying to nail the closet door shut so it would hold for another four years, he was trying to pry the nails out with his bare fingers just so he could be free.

My entire future relationship with Daryl was hanging in the balance on this single moment. How I reacted would change everything between us, and I was not about to screw it up.

"Then he's a loser," I said, and flashed him a warm smile.

"You're not bothered by it?" Daryl asked with both surprise and uncertainty. I could understand both of those.

"I love you and I want what I would want for you if you were straight. For you to be happy, healthy and loved. That's all that matters to me. Whether I stand next to you at the end of the aisle as you marry a woman or a man, it's all the same to me. All I care about is being there and seeing that smile on your face."

"That's all I want for you, too. Even if it's with someone as annoying as Kayla," Daryl said with a smirk.

I couldn't stop the groan from escaping. "Yeah, I don't know what to do about that. I know she's into me, but I just can't imagine spending the rest of my life with her. I gotta figure out how to let her down gently or make it seem like it was her idea and she dumps me before we even date."

"Good luck with that. Both of our fathers seem pretty hell bent on it. Maybe you should take her on a date to help feed the homeless or something. She doesn't really come across as the giving back kind of a girl."

"She is a princess."

I had to agree with him on that one. Kayla was the type that showed up dressed for a gala every time you saw her. High-end clothes, hair and makeup professionally done. It didn't matter if she was just running to the grocery store—not that I believed she actually did her own grocery shopping—she still always dressed to impress. I knew there were guys who liked that kind of woman. A trophy wife. The problem is, even if I was into girls, Kayla wouldn't be it. I was going to have to figure out how to squash this before it went too far. I just wasn't sure how to make that happen yet.

I bumped my shoulder against Daryl's as I spoke. "Come on, let's get in there before we get in trouble for being late to our own dinner party. Tomorrow we can brainstorm some ideas on how to make Brad pay."

"Deal," Daryl said with a genuine smile.

It would hurt for a little while, but I knew he would bounce back soon enough. The first time your heart gets broken, it's always hard, but then you get tougher and learn how to protect yourself better. He was going to be okay, because I was going to make sure of it.

CHAPTER THREE

Jimmy

NEVER, EVER AGAIN. And I do mean never again. When I agreed to go on this blind date, it was completely due to peer pressure. I love my friends, but they seriously suck at finding men for me. Ali and Kristy had good intentions, I know they love me, but this has to stop. They kept going on and on about how I needed to find me a man to date. Like being eighteen meant I was destined to be alone for the rest of my life if I was single come graduation. Don't get me wrong, I get that we're high school seniors and on the cusp of starting our adult lives. I completely understand how we should be having fun, dating, going to parties, thinking about prom, and I do all of that. But, I also have zero desire to be a drunken idiot when I go away to College. Yes, a boyfriend would be amazing, but that wasn't a top priority in my life. I needed to focus on my grades to ensure my scholarship and my acceptance into Maryland Institute College of Art was bulletproof. Yes, I had already received the scholarship and acceptance, but that could be taken away if my grades fall, something I wasn't going to allow. So, tonight marks the very last night that I am going to be entertaining any of my friends with dating. There will be absolutely zero future blind dates.

I headed into my house and saw that my parents were waiting up for me. My parents had always been amazing, but tonight they deserved an award for saving me like they did. One simple text message asking for 9-1-1 help and they were calling up saying I needed to get home, that my dog was very sick.

God I love them.

Whiskers instantly came running over to me with his tail wagging. My parents had surprised me with him when I was thirteen and Whiskers had been my best friend ever since. He was a mutt that they rescued from the shelter when he was only eight weeks old. I didn't care that he was all mixed up. To me, he was perfect. He was a good, medium size dog that loved to spend the hot summer months in the kiddie pool in our backyard. He was my dog and I was going to miss him when I would be off staying at the dorms.

"He's made a miraculous recovery," my mom said with a big smile.

"God, you have no idea how amazing you are," I said as I collapsed into the chair.

"It couldn't have been that bad," my Dad said.

"I would have rather spent the night scrubbing the bathrooms at the diner with my own toothbrush."

"That's bad. Was he a jerk?" my Mom asked, the concern in her voice evident.

"More like a pompous air head. Honestly, I have no idea how he managed to get his head into his shirt. He spent the night talking about himself and how great he is. And then, when I did get to talk, the conversation was remedial at best. He's an idiot, and I say that in the nicest way possible."

"That's too bad. I'm sorry you had such a bad time tonight. Maybe next time hold your ground with your friends," my Dad advised. And he was absolutely right.

"Oh, believe me, they will be getting an earful from me come Monday morning. I need to get this night out of me, so I am going to go and paint for a bit," I said as I stood.

"Okay, sweetie. We're going to head to bed, so don't stay up too late," my Mom said as they both stood as well.

"I won't. I love you guys."

"We love you, too," my Dad said, a warm smile turning up the corners of his mouth.

We all headed upstairs and into our respective rooms. After I quickly changed into some old jeans and a t-shirt, I made my way back down the stairs and into the garage.

The garage was another reason why I loved my parents so much. Not only had they accepted me as being gay, but they also accepted my passion for art. My dad had converted the garage into my own art studio. I couldn't believe it when I came home from school three years ago to see it. My dad had always kept his car in the garage so he could work on it. He constantly called it his man cave, and he had given that up so I could have a place to pursue my passion, my future career. I couldn't have loved him more.

I grabbed a new canvas and started the process of grabbing different paints. I needed to paint away this night to cleanse my heart and soul. Dylan needed to go away.

As I moved the brush over the canvas, I allowed myself to think back to last night and meeting Zane at the diner. I still couldn't get his face out of my mind. The way his eyes seemed to track me as I moved from table to table.

I knew being a new manager it would be natural for him to keep an eye on his employees. To see how they were working, see how they interacted with customers. It made sense and Zane wasn't the first new manager that I'd had at the diner.

Still, I couldn't stop thinking about him. I couldn't stop wondering if maybe his eyes were on me for another reason. I wasn't sure, but I could have sworn there was lust in his eyes when he saw me bending over to wipe the tables. It was gone, though, before I could really confirm it one way or the other.

It should have been creepy and disturbing and I'm sure it would have if he wasn't so sexy. If he was a forty year old man, it would have given me the creeps. But Zane wasn't forty, he was twenty-one, from what we were able to gather out of him. We couldn't get much more out of him. We had no idea if he was dating someone, if he was straight, gay, in College, literally nothing. The man was like Fort Knox in the sharing department. It should have told me to back off, but I couldn't help but think about how sexy he was, the mystery about him was not helping either. I was in so much trouble, because he was my manager, which made him my boss and I could not oogle my boss all night long.

What I did in my fantasies, though, was well within my freedom. I wish I knew if he was straight or gay. That would really help me to be able to figure him out. If he was straight, then he was just another manager. But if he was gay, then he was attracted to me. Didn't mean anything could happen, because, again, he's my manager, but it was a fun thought.

Maybe Ali and Kristy were right, maybe I needed someone to have some fun with. Dylan was not it, but maybe I should be trying to get out. I could certainly use the sex, I'd always been able to paint more freely if I wasn't stressed or tense and sex was the best stress reliever in the world. Maybe it was time I lived a little, and tonight I would be doing just that with Zane.

In my dreams anyway.

***

There was nothing better than spending my Saturday in the art supply store. I could seriously live here and never get tired of it. There was a peacefulness to being in an art store.

Most just see paint, brushes, pencils and blank canvases. But to me, I see what they could become. I see the sunset with a bend of yellows, reds, and oranges that rests upon the water. I see the tranquility it brings, the warmth it brings within a household. How the owner picks it because it matches their lives or simply because they need it in their lives.

It's so much more than just liquid color in a bottle. It's what it makes a person feel when the masterpiece has been created. It's those feelings that make it all worth it for an artist, knowing that we brought that level of emotion out in someone. It's the biggest compliment that any artist could have.

Just as I turned the corner, I instantly hit a wall. Only this wall was not made of wood and paint, but hard and warm flesh. Looking up to apologize immediately, I was shocked to see it was none other than Zane.

"Hey, sorry," I said, as I tried to get

my mind to work. My boss was standing here in an art supply store and he was looking as sexy as ever. He was wearing dark blue jeans with a black t-shirt and a black leather jacket. I couldn't help but wonder if maybe he had a motorcycle. The image immediately popped up in my mind of him sitting on a motorcycle and it had my mouth watering.

God, I gotta get a grip.

"Don't worry about it, I wasn't paying attention. Are you okay?" Zane asked, flashing me an easy smile.

"Oh yeah, I'm fine." Aside from the heart attack. "I didn't know you were into art."

"Oh, I'm not. I can barely draw stick figures. My kid brother, Daryl, is the artist in the family. He just got dumped so I figured I would get him a couple of things to help cheer him up."

That made more sense. I didn't get artist vibes from Zane, but it was sweet he was grabbing stuff for his brother. He was compassionate, a very good quality in a man.

"That sucks that he was dumped. Painting it out, though, can really help."

"I'm assuming that means you paint."

"Since I can remember. My mom says I was born with a paint brush in my hand. They have been really great about it. My dad even turned the garage into an art studio for me a few years ago," I said proudly.

God I love my parents.

"That's awesome. Are you gonna go to art school when you graduate?"

"I've already received an acceptance

to MICA, Maryland Institute College of Art. It's in Baltimore. I'm so excited for it, it's going to be amazing," I said with a smile so big I must have looked like a psychotic person, but I didn't care. The excitement at getting to go to MICA was exploding inside of me. I doubted it would ever get old.

"That's awesome, Jimmy. Why so close, though? Don't you want to be as far away from this town as possible?"

He wasn't the first person to ask me this. When people think of art, their minds go to New York or California. They don't go to Baltimore, all of thirty minutes up the road from here. I know it was close and, yes, I could have applied for other schools in New York or Los Angeles, but I didn't want to. I didn't want to be thousands of miles away.

"I like this town, for starters, but more importantly, I wanted to be close to home. I don't have any siblings or relatives. It's just me and my folks. I wanted to be close to them, still. To be able to drive home for family dinners or holidays. I didn't want to have to book a plane ticket just to come home for the weekend. And MICA is an amazing art school with unbelievable resources. I get to have a wonderful education while still being able to be close to home."

"Sounds like the best of both worlds for you. Think you can lend me some expertise on figuring out what to get my brother?" Zane said with wink and a grin.

Oh damn.

"I would love to." Any extra time outside of work that I could get to spend with him, I was going to be taking it.

"You are a lifesaver. Maybe if you have time afterward, we could grab some lunch," Zane offered.

"Sure." I couldn't stop the smile this time. I would not only get to be helping him in a place I considered heaven on earth, but I would get to sit with him for lunch, too. This day was turning out way better than I could have ever imagined. And trust me, I can imagine a hell of a lot.

***

We ended up at just a little cafe not too far from the art supply store. They had amazing pastries and some of the best coffee I'd ever had. Despite really wanting to just order sugar confections, I forced myself to order a ham and swiss sandwich along with my pastry.

Spring was fully in the air and I was relieved for the warmth it brought. We sat outside with how balmy it was. I couldn't help but notice how the sunlight played with the different shades of brown within Zane's hair. It was all natural, but it looked like he paid a few hundred dollars for highlights in it. The brown in his hair only made his emerald green eyes shimmer even more and I knew I could easily get lost in them.

"So, do you like working at the diner?" I wasn't really sure how to get the conversation going. If I was sitting with my friends we would have already been talking up a storm. Zane was different, though, he was new in my life, my manager, older, and I still had no idea if he was gay or straight. Not that the last one truly mattered, but it would have been nice to know.

"So far, yes. It's only temporary, but it's decent work."

"Why only temporary?"

"I wanted some hands-on experience working with hospitality in a management position. It also allows me to pay for my tuition to the online hospitality management course I'm taking."

"That's cool. Why didn't you go to a physical College compared to online?" Most people jump at the opportunity to get out of town. For someone his age, it would only make sense that he would leave home and get some life experience with being in College and living on his own. I guess he could be living on his own in town, not everyone lives with their parents here. He might have had to stay so he could help his parents and be there for his kid brother.

"My father didn't see it as being necessary. He preferred for me to work for his company, but I wanted real life experience first, before working for his pharmaceutical company."

"That makes sense. It must be hard to have parents who own a corporation. Most would assume you would want to be in that company, to pass it on to you. You obviously want to be within the hospitality industry. What's your dream?"

I was very lucky in the sense that my parents worked medium income jobs. They didn't own a business. My mother was a grade school teacher and my father was an accountant at the only firm in town. There was no pressure for me to join the family business or have to take over one day. I was completely free to be myself and chase after my own dreams without any guilt. It seemed like Zane didn't have that, and that was truly sad.

"I would like to open a resort, similar to one you would find in Las Vegas or other vacation destination locations. Something that would bring tourists into the town to help other local businesses. I want something that can withstand the test of time and be something I can be proud of and pass on to my children, should they wish it. Mostly, I just want something that is mine and not connected to generations of Hamiltons."

Oh, that's right, he's a Hamilton. They own a massive pharmaceutical empire. That explained a few things. I could tell even with how he was talking that he was expected to take over the family business. That there was pressure from his parents to take it over. Pressure like that could be crippling to someone, I would imagine. Still, though, he was pushing through it and chasing after his own dreams. It was admiral and impressive.

"I don't have a family business or generations of high expectations. I can't imagine how hard that must be for you to deal with. I'm lucky in that sense. My parents have always encouraged me to pursue my dreams and carve out my own life. I think it's impressive and very brave of you to chase after your dream and go against the wishes of your family. You shouldn't have to feel like you need to conform to what they want. They got to live their lives, it's your turn to live yours so you can be happy."

The warm smile that spread across his face had my stomach filling with butterflies. I'd seen him smile before at work plenty of times, but this was different. This wasn't some polite smile you gave to someone you just met or because you had to. This was a genuine and true smile. It lit up his face. And his eyes became even more green, if that was even possible.

"Your parents sound like really amazing people."

"They are the best. I won the lottery with them, seriously. They are completely supportive of me wanting to be an artist, where most parents would be trying to convince me to get a *real* job.

And when I came out at fourteen, they just said, "we know", and asked what I wanted for dinner. They didn't bat an eye when I brought my first boyfriend home, or object if I ever need to talk to them about something. They've always been supportive and I know that makes me very lucky. I've heard and seen firsthand some horror stories with people coming out to their parents. My one friend got kicked out, but thankfully, he had an older brother who had his own apartment and was very accepting of him."

I couldn't take my eyes away from his face. I was used to telling people I was gay and there was always a reaction. People couldn't help it, the second they heard it there was either shock, disgust, confusion, or complete acceptance on their face and within their eyes.

To me, I am who I am, and I don't care to change. But depending on how you react would dictate how our interactions would be. If you didn't like that I was gay, well you and I were never going to be talking again. It was just that simple to me and there were people I hadn't spoken with again because of it.

I was relieved to see no form of disgust within his eyes. There was a calm understanding there. But what was also interesting, for a second I could have sworn there was lust. Once again, this man was giving me mixed feelings. One second, I am confident he was straight and then he would look at me a certain way and my confidence would go right out the window. I had to know if he was gay or not. I couldn't keep playing this guessing game any longer. It was going to drive me insane.

"So, are you dating anyone?" I asked with a lot more bravery then I was feeling.

"No, I'm single. You?" he said with a small smirk.

That so did not answer my question at all. It wasn't like I could just flat out ask him if he got turned on by guys or girls. That smirk told me that he was toying with me. I would almost say flirting slightly. That coy answer was designed to keep me wondering and it was going to drive me crazy. He had no idea how much it was going to bother me not knowing the answer officially. Hell, maybe he was bi-sexual. No matter the direction he swung, he seemed to be enjoying torturing me.

"Single, and if the blind date that I was dragged into going on last night was anything to go by, I'll be single for a while," I answered as the waitress brought our food over.

"Why, was he that ugly?"

I gave a small laugh at that. Dylan would have been very attractive if he didn't talk. "No, that wasn't his problem."

I told him all about how pompous and self-centered the guy was. We both had fun laughing about it and talking about other people we'd known who had been downright terrible.

The conversation between us flowed so seamlessly and smooth. It was as if we had been friends for years compared to only knowing each other less than forty-eight hours. He was smart and funny. He was not boring at all and he could listen, too. He had no problem sitting there listening to my stories and adding his own input to them. It felt amazing.

We had talked for so long that by the time we left, it was almost dinner time. We had been talking for four hours, but it only felt like minutes. We had exchanged numbers and were going to meet tomorrow to go bowling. I wasn't really a bowler, but I was willing to do anything if it meant I could see Zane again.

We were building a friendship and I knew that even if he was straight, a friendship with Zane was a hell of a lot better than nothing at all. He was a good man and he was someone I wanted in my life. Now, I just had to make sure my attraction to him didn't turn into a full-blown crush.

At least, not until I discovered if he was gay or not.

CHAPTER FOUR

Zane

THE LAST FEW weeks had been a mixture of emotions for me. The pressure coming from my father was getting intense, more so than it had been previously. He was constantly asking me about Kayla and talking about the company. He was not pleased with me working at the diner and he would often ask me when I was going to quit and come work for a *real* company. Thankfully, he was still completely in the dark about my online courses. I could only imagine the explosion that would come out of him if he discovered my secret.

It was ridiculous when I thought about it. I shouldn't have to hide my education from my own parents. I shouldn't have to keep this as a secret from him. Going to school, wanting to better my education, shouldn't be something that I had to treat as a secret. I shouldn't have to hide it like I'm selling drugs on the street corner. The fact that I couldn't let my parents know about my courses only solidified that I could never tell them about being gay, not until I was twenty-five. They would kick me out and disown me, not that it would bother me all that much, but I wasn't going to lose my inheritance. I had earned that money and it was set for my future. I couldn't risk losing it.

Aside from my inheritance, I couldn't risk Daryl and his safety. I wasn't worried about his physical health, but his mental and emotional health I was worried about. He was gay, and apparently more open about it than me, if our conversation was anything to go by. He wasn't going to make it until he was twenty-five in that house. He was seventeen, soon to be eighteen in three months, so if my parents discovered he was gay they would be free to kick him out. He would have nothing. He'd be a senior in high school living on the street. I had to be there for him. I had to make it four more years so he would have a safety net. So he could come out in four years and not have to fear being homeless. He would have a place to stay with me, where he would be free to be himself and to chance his own dreams. We would have to fight so he could keep his inheritance, but that was a fight we could face together.

The highlight of the past few weeks had been my time with Jimmy. He was the light in the very dark tunnel that I was trapped in. We had been able to spend most days together, even if it was just grabbing a meal together or working together. Seeing Jimmy made all of the sneaking around and frustrations worth it. Seeing him was like getting fresh air. He was breathing life back into a dying man and, fuck, I needed the breaths.

There was one hiccup, though. The more time I spent with him, the more I was haunted by him. His face would invade my dreams, my fantasies. I would wake up as hard as a rock and no amount of cold showers would make it go back down. The only way I could get rid of my erection was to jerk off. The dirty little things we would do in my fantasies...

Fuck, I couldn't think about that now or I would be hard at work.

The one thing I truly admired about him was how easy it was for him to just be himself. He was so open and accepting of who he was. He was gay and he was very proud of it. He didn't have to hide. He was free to be out and proud. His parents loved him and supported him in not only his sexual orientation, but his dreams.

God, my father would shit a brick if I went to him and asked if we could turn the garage into a paint studio. He hated that Daryl loved to paint and draw. To him that was feminine and completely unacceptable for a man.

Jimmy had the kind of parents that everyone dreamed of having. The kind *I* always dreamed of having. I was happy for him, don't get me wrong, but it only confirmed how screwed up my family truly was.

Letting out a sigh as the last customer of the night left, I made my way over and locked the door before turning off the open light. It was only me and Jimmy left tonight to get everything closed up.

Normally, I would be very happy with

that outcome, but tonight had been rough. Everything going on with my father, plus my growing desire for Jimmy, didn't make me very good company tonight. Something needed to give. I knew my father wasn't going to, which meant my attraction to Jimmy needed to. The problem was, you couldn't just turn it on and off. There wasn't some light switch in my head that I could flip to end an attraction. If there was, I could be straight and have one less thing to worry about in my life.

"Are you okay? You've been quiet and a bit broody all shift," Jimmy asked from behind the counter, concern shining in his eyes.

Oh my God, this guy is so amazing.

I guess broody was the right word for it. Normally, at work me and him would talk and joke around. I'm more free to be myself there, but tonight I couldn't shake off the frustrations from life. I had been more quiet and kept to myself. Focused on some work in the back office and basically avoided people. It wasn't how I liked to run my shift.

"Sorry," I said, as I got the blinds all closed off.

"Don't be, but you can talk to me you know."

I made my way over behind the counter as Jimmy removed his server's pouch and started to get everything put away. We only had one customer in the diner for the past hour, so most of the closing jobs had already been done.

It had been a slow night tonight, something I was also grateful for. I knew I could talk with him, but I also knew he was still trying to figure out if I was straight or gay. I suspected he knew I was gay. He had caught me looking at his lips way too many times. I couldn't help it, though. They looked so kissable. We hadn't talked about dating, really, outside of that one conversation a few weeks ago. That was focused on Jimmy's horrible blind date and it had nothing to do with my love life, or lack thereof.

I had other friends, but those were the friends picked by my father as being *suitable* for our family. They were all the same, stuck up rich guys that talked way too much about which girl they were banging. They weren't people that I could talk to about Kayla and how I felt about her. They would not only *not* be interested in any of my feelings, but they also wouldn't understand. To them, a girl like Kayla was perfect. She would look good on your arm, she would put out as much as you wanted and wouldn't care if you cheated on her as long as she got to spend money. I couldn't talk to anyone, but maybe I could talk to Jimmy about it. Maybe, I could finally unload my thoughts and feelings on the situation I was being forced into.

"I had to go out on a first date with this girl, Kayla," I started. I wanted to see how he reacted to the news that I was "straight". If he seemed a bit confused, then that would tell me he suspected I was gay, so discovering that I was gay wouldn't be a shock. It was putting off the inevitable, I was aware of that, but it would help for me to know that I was making the right decision in telling him.

"Oh, did it not go well?" he asked, and flashed a sort of half-smile.

The tone in his voice and that look of 'trying to appear happy but not really feeling it' told me everything I needed to know. He wasn't fully shocked, but he was disappointed. He might not have known if I was gay one hundred percent, but he'd been hoping I was. It seemed like I wasn't the only one with an attraction between us.

"It was terrible. *She* is terrible, and I know that sounds bad, but she is really terrible. A complete airhead and self-centered. The whole dinner I had to keep reminding myself that I couldn't stab her with the salad fork."

"Wow, a salad fork, eh? Very fancy for a first date," Jimmy teased.

"Not my idea. She comes from old money so she expects a certain level of luxury. Which does not help her case at all."

"If you didn't like her, then why ask her out?"

It was a very simple question, one that should have had a simple answer, but this one really didn't.

"You know how my father runs a pharmaceutical company, but what I didn't tell you was that it's Hamilton Pharmaceuticals. It's been in my family for generations so I come from old money. My father has been trying to make a deal with another company that owns fifty hospitals all across the country. It would be serious revenue and profit for the company if they can secure the deal. Kayla Miller is the daughter of the current owner, Henry Miller."

"Ah, so he wants you and her to get together to help solidify the deal. If his daughter is dating you, and if you are making her happy, then that will help persuade him into signing a contract," Jimmy said with complete understanding.

"Exactly. He wants me to date her and eventually marry her. He doesn't care what I want. He doesn't care if I'm attracted to her or if we're even a good fit. All my father cares about is expanding the company. To him, my being with Kayla is a sacrifice I should be honored to make."

And that was the thing, my father should have asked what I thought of her. Even if I was straight, he shouldn't have assumed I would be attracted to her. He should have pulled me aside and talked to me like a normal father would have and asked what I thought about her. Asked me if I could see myself being with her for the rest of my life. He didn't, though, because to him it was just another line in a contract. I was something he could use to better a deal. He didn't care, not one bit about me, and that really hurt.

"Well, what do you want, then?" Jimmy asked gently.

It was a simple and innocent question, but it was one I hadn't really heard all that often. Everyone told me what I was expected to do. No one tended to ask me what I wanted. This might be a mistake, but I think the bigger mistake would be to let this moment pass me by. If I was going to regret this night, I want it to because I took action instead of doing nothing.

Before I could change my mind or chicken out, I was moving. As I moved closer to him, Jimmy moved back. I kept going until his back hit the counter. Placing my hands on either side of him on the counter, I spoke.

"I want you." Without giving him a chance to say anything, I pressed my lips against his. The second our lips made contact there was an explosion of fire that spread through my entire body. It was like nothing I had ever felt before. Something as simple as a kiss should not leave me feeling like this. The gentle press of his lips back against mine had me instantly hard. The kiss was simple and he was uncertain, I could feel that in his hesitation against my own lips.

But he wasn't pulling back. I wanted more of him. I needed more of him, but before I could deepen the kiss, he was pulling back.

CHAPTER FIVE

Jimmy

HE KISSED ME.

Zane kissed me.

Holy shit.

I needed to think. I needed time to consider what all of this could mean. But, I couldn't think, because all I could get my mind to focus on was how amazing it felt to have his lips against mine. The same lips that were millimeters apart from my very own right now.

Screw thinking, it's overrated.

Grabbing the front of his shirt, I pulled him back to me, crushing our lips back together. This time, though, the kiss was anything but light and gentle. The gloves were off and we were both allowing our attraction to the other to explode.

Zane easily dominated the kiss and I was more than happy to allow him. Once I felt his tongue against my lips, seeking permission, I easily granted him it. I parted my lips so his tongue could dance with mine.

The second his tongue reached mine I couldn't help the moan that crept from my throat. Kissing was one of my favorite parts. There was just something about it that told me everything I needed to know about the man I was with. If it sent a shiver down my spine, I knew the attraction, the chemistry, was going to be off the wall. If he was gentle and hesitant, then I knew he was going to be uncertain about every step that came after.

Zane's kiss, though, not only did it send shockwave after shockwave of electricity all over my body, but his kiss was confident and strong. He knew exactly what he wanted and he was not holding back or afraid to go after it.

The need to feel his skin against mine became too great. I needed to touch him. Pressing my hands to his chest, I casually trailed my fingers over his warm pecs, down to his rippled stomach, and then up underneath his shirt.

Zane apparently felt the same because before I even knew it, he had my shirt open and off, leaving me in just my jeans. This was stupid, I knew messing around with my new boss could end things for me at the diner, but I didn't care. I couldn't think of anything else but feeling Zane against me.

I quickly removed his shirt, pushing it off his shoulders as Zane broke the kiss and peppered his way up my neck to the sensitive spot below my ear, causing me to moan once more. I tilted my head back to grant him better access to my neck as shivers flared up and down my spine.

His hands went to my ass and he pulled me closer, tighter against his hips. The second our hard cocks rubbed against each other, even through our jeans, it was pure bliss. Both of us moaned deeply and I started at the electrified sensation that shot through my belly to my balls.

"I need you," Zane said in a breathy voice that vibrated against my lips. In this moment that was the only thing I needed to hear.

"Fuck, yes," I breathed back.

It was like a switch had been flipped at my simple confirmation. Zane's hands were everywhere, all over my body. The need we both felt was explosive. The desperation to feel the other's skin against our own bodies took over all logic and reason.

My hands were instantly going to his pants, quickly undoing them so I could free his hard cock. It felt huge trapped within his jeans and the need to see it, to feel it with my own hand, was all I could think about. I was rewarded with not only a large and solid cock within my hand, but Zane let loose a deep, throaty moan at the contact.

He made quick work of divesting me of my pants. I kicked off my shoes, allowing him to pull the jeans off each foot and toss them to the floor. Once I was completely naked, I was expecting to feel Zane's hand on my cock. Only, I was pleasantly surprised when he dropped to his knees, licked his lips, and then gave my engorged tip a lick, slurping up the white pearl of pre-cum that had gathered at the slit.

I couldn't stop my eyes from fluttering shut as intense pleasure scorched through me. I couldn't stop the cry that slipped from my lips as his hot mouth took my cock all the way down to the base. Clearly, he was very good at this.

Zane moved my left leg up so it was sitting on one of the shelves behind the counter to give him better access. I opened my eyes and looked down as he worked my cock with his full lips. The sight of it was almost enough to make me come.

Zane pulled back off me with an audible *pop*. Licking his lips, he reached into his pants pocket and pulled out his wallet. He dug around for a brief moment, and then tugged out a condom and a small packet of lube.

I wasn't going to allow myself to think about why he would have those in his wallet. Zane wasn't going to even give me the chance to think about it, because he was once again taking me all the way down to my base, his moans reverberating through my shaft and into my balls, driving me dangerously close to the edge already. The vibrations had me whimpering from the pleasure. My eyes closed again and I surrendered myself to Zane's magical tongue.

When I felt his finger tracing cool lube over my puckered hole, excitement shot through me. I couldn't wait until I could feel him inside of me. Until I could feel his cock buried balls deep within me. I was a very happy bottom. I knew some guys who liked to switch back and forth, but for me, I was a definite bottom. I had zero desire to be a top and I loved to bottom far too much to give it up.

Zane worked his two and then three fingers quickly inside of me, stretching me enough so that he would fit. His mouth was moving slower on my cock, and I knew he was trying to hold me off. I wanted to come so badly, but I wanted him to be buried inside of me when I did.

"Zane, please, fuck me." A deep moan escaped me as his fingers hit my sweet spot and stars danced across my eyes.

I don't know if it was the moan or what I said, but Zane didn't need any more incentive to move things along. He slowly pulled his fingers out and the next second I was laying flat against the counter and Zane was in between my legs.

"It's gonna be hard and fast," Zane warned and I knew he was teetering on the edge along with me.

"Fuck yes," I easily agreed. That was the only way I wanted this to go. Don't get me wrong, I've got no problem with slow and sweet, but tonight I wanted it hard and fast. I was a volcano waiting to blow and I needed to explode.

Zane quickly rolled on the condom and then I finally felt his tip against my ass. He pushed in slowly. Even though I was stretched, he was so big there was still a slight sting to it. I didn't care, though, because the second his tip breached my opening the world shattered all around me. Inch by inch, he pushed inside of me, going deeper and deeper than any guy had ever gone before. His cock was large and long and it felt glorious inside of me. By the time he was all the way down to his base, we were both breathing heavy.

"You okay?" Zane asked.

"I'll be better once you move."

Zane flashed me a sexy smirk and he kept his eyes on mine as he slowly pulled out almost all of the way before he snapped his hips forward, burying himself deep inside of me again. The sensation and pleasure had me arching my back and moaning, only fueling him on. Zane kept true to his word and fucked me hard, fast, and deep. When the tip of his cock hit my sweet spot all control went right out the window.

"Zane," I moaned as I wrapped my legs around his hips.

Zane continued to hit my sweet spot dead on with each thrust. The contact and friction was bringing me closer and closer to my release. I was a moaning mess on the counter, but I wasn't the only one. Zane's moans bounced off the walls of the diner as his own need for release was fast approaching.

"Come for me, baby," Zane said, as the walls of my ass started to tighten around him.

I was so close, so fucking close, and with one final direct hit on my prostate, I was all but screaming Zane's name as I came hard, spurting hot, white ropes of cum over my belly.

The tightening of my walls around Zane's cock pushed him over the edge and I was blissfully rewarded with feeling him pulsing inside of me. My whole body was tingling. I was still coming, something that was remarkable all in itself. It was rare when I was able to come from sex without my dick being touched. Zane had a serious talent and I had a feeling it was one I would never grow tired of.

The only sound in the diner was the sound of our heavy breathing. I knew I should be moving, but I wasn't fully confident that my legs would be able to hold my weight right now. That was easily the best sex of my life. I could still feel Zane pulsing inside of me and it was complete bliss.

Zane gave me a very sweet and slow kiss before he pulled back and slowly pulled out of me with a groan. He moved back and quickly removed the condom and tossed it into the garbage before he turned his attention to me. I slowly sat up, the room spinning for a second. I wasn't worried about it, though. I knew it was from breathing so heavy. I just needed to get my breathing back to normal.

"Are you okay? I didn't hurt you?"

Zane asked, slightly concerned with how fast he had gone.

"Fuck no. That was amazing. I don't think I can walk right now," I said with a goofy smile.

I knew this was all going to click in soon, but right now I was just going to enjoy the after bliss I was in right now. The sexy smirk Zane shot my way sent a shiver down my spine. This man was sex on a stick.

Zane got his clothes back on and went to take the garbage out to the dumpster. By the time he got back, I had managed to get dressed and to stand. We were basically done with closing and now we were starting to reach the slightly awkward part of sleeping with someone for the first time. I mean, was this a one-night stand type of deal? He said he wanted me and the way he could suck cock and fuck told me it was not his first time being with a man. Yet, he was dating a girl, or supposed to be, so what did it all mean?

"Why don't you grab your bag and I'll give you a ride home," Zane suggested.

All I could do was nod to that and head off into the back to grab my backpack. It took everything in me to not comment that he already gave me one hell of a ride.

I quickly grabbed my bag and headed out with him. We got into his car, and after telling him my address, we were off.

Awkward didn't seem to cut it for the first five minutes of the drive. I wanted to say something, but I wasn't sure what to say. I wanted to know what this all meant, but at the same time I was afraid of the answer. If he said it was only a one-time thing, I would have to accept that and go back to working around him. It would suck, though.

"I don't want this to be a one-night stand. If that is what you want, then I'll respect it, but I'm hoping that isn't what you want." Zane's voice snapped me out of my thoughts and for a moment I had to make sure he actually said the words and it wasn't my imagination.

"I'm not a one-night stand type of guy. I like you. I just don't know what you want. I mean, you said you were dating that Kayla girl."

And technically, he just cheated on her with me. Not good. I was the dirty mistress in this situation, not something I ever thought I would be.

"We aren't officially dating, I've never

even kissed her or held her hand, and I have no plans of doing either with her. I like you, Jimmy. I'm gay, but I'm in the closet only because of my parents. If they discovered I was gay they would not only kick me out, which I wouldn't care all that much, but they would also remove my inheritance. I need that money for my dream. Once I turn twenty-five, it automatically goes to me and there is nothing they can do or say to change that. I just need to go another four years without them finding out I'm gay. Afterward, I don't have to hide anymore. And I know it's a lot to ask someone who is out and proud to be kept in the shadows, and if you can't handle that or don't want to, I completely understand. I would never hold it against you. But if you are okay with that, if you want to pursue something with me, then I'd really like to take you out on a date."

A date?

Could I really go out with him on a date knowing I would have to be a secret he keeps for the next four years?

Yes, four years was a long way away and anything could happen between now and then. Hell, in three months we might not even still be together.

What could one date really hurt, right?

"I'd like that."

The big smile that Zane sent my way told me everything I needed to know. He really did have feelings for me. Maybe this would turn out to be a terrible idea, but for right now it didn't seem like such a bad idea. Sex at work on the other hand, though, not the best idea I've had.

"Great, I'll text you in a couple of days and we can figure something out with our work schedule."

I just gave a nod and then enjoyed the silence between us. It was no longer awkward, but now a comfortable silence, something I was very pleased about. I didn't live that far from the diner, so it only took another ten minutes before we were pulling up front of my house.

"Thanks for the ride," I said as I removed my seatbelt.

"No problem. I'll text you tomorrow."

"Goodnight, Zane."

I wanted to kiss him, but he seemed to be unsure about it. I could see his eyes darting around the area to see if anyone was watching us. I was starting to get a picture of what it might be like if

I did date him.

"Night, Jimmy," he said with a warm, rich smile. It was a nice smile, don't get me wrong, but I would have preferred a goodnight kiss.

Accepting that it wasn't going to happen, I got out of his car and quickly made my way inside, relieved that my parents were already in bed. Once I was safely in my room, I couldn't help but slowly sink down to the floor with my back pressed against the door. Shock. I could safely say I was in shock. It was a good shock, don't get me wrong, but shock nonetheless. Never have I ever had sex in a public place before, much less my work. Thankfully, there were no cameras at the diner so we weren't going to be fired. I could only imagine the rumors about that going around town.

SHATTERED

In a town this size, the rumor mill was always turning. There was always someone that was sleeping with some married person. Always some scandal that was going around, and with Zane being in the closet, the last thing he needed was for the whole town to hear about him having sex on the counter in the diner.

I can't believe I did that. I had never done anything like that before. Anytime I've had sex it was always behind closed doors. A closed *bedroom* door. I've never done anything out in public. Well, I've kissed, but never anything more. I don't know what happened. One second we're talking, then the next his lips were on mine and it was like my mind completely shut off. All logic and reason went right out the window.

I needed him.

I had never needed someone that badly before. I had never had a desire for another person that strong before. It was like my whole body was on fire and his hands were the only thing that could put it out. I could still feel his hands lingering all over my body. His scent was covering my skin and it was intoxicating. My body was craving him, craving his touch all over again. If I wasn't careful I could become addicted to his touch and that wasn't something I could afford.

I swore I would never be with someone that was in the closet again. That I wouldn't put myself in the position of where I would have to hide who I am with. I couldn't hide who I was, most people knew I was gay, but I wasn't the type that enjoyed having to be some dirty secret. I wanted to be shown off. I wanted to see the proud smile on my boyfriend's face when he introduced me. I wanted kisses and hand holding. I wanted it all, and being with someone in the closet took it all away. Save those kisses and moments for when we were alone. Having to hide in the closet with someone was not something I was looking to do. And yet, here I was actually thinking about it. Actually agreeing to going out on a date with him. It was absurd and chances were this was only going to end in tears. My tears. Even though I know all of that, I was still going to go through with the date. I wanted him, I had wanted him from the very first second he walked into the diner. I never thought he would be gay, much less interested in me, but he was.

Maybe this would turn out to be a mistake, but it was my mistake to make and I had to take the risk.

I would be protecting my heart, though. I was taking a huge risk by going out with him. I understand why he has to hide, why he can't come out, I truly do, but I also needed to keep myself safe. I had to protect my heart, because chances were, this relationship was going to go down in flames and when the smoke cleared it would be me left heartbroken in the soot.

CHAPTER SIX

Zane

THIS WAS INSANE. I couldn't be this nervous about something as simple as a first date. I had been on plenty of first dates. Well, not plenty, but enough to make me anything but a novice. Still, here I was standing in front of my mirror after changing my outfit eight times. It was ridiculous, and yet here I was in my ninth outfit trying to convince myself that I looked good.

All of this was crazy. We had already had sex. At work, on the counter, admittedly not the best idea, but if it was a mistake it was the best mistake I had ever made. This wasn't my first time having a one-night stand, but generally those guys were the ones I picked up in the bar. They weren't someone that I wanted to date. Someone that I wanted to have conversations with and to curl up on the couch with.

Jimmy, he could be that person. He's different, he's smart and funny and very creative. He is so free to be himself and he embraces every aspect of himself. He shares who he is to this world and I wanted that. I couldn't wait until I could have that.

Letting out a deep breath and giving myself one last look in the mirror, I headed out of my room and made my way down the stairs. I moved quickly in order to avoid running into my father. The last thing I needed tonight was to see him. I was in a good mood and he would only ruin it.

"Zane."

Of course.

I was almost at the door.

I was so close.

Another ten feet and I would have been free from him. I quickly turned around, hoping to get this over and done with so I could leave. The last thing I wanted to be was late for tonight. It wasn't anything special, just going to the movies, but still. It was our time together and I didn't want to miss a single second of it.

"Father."

"I have just finished speaking with Henry. Kayla has been enjoying your time together, though she wishes it was more often."

Great.

There was a lecture coming. I could see it all over his face and hear it in his tone. He wasn't happy that Kayla wasn't getting enough of me. That she wasn't getting more of my time. The problem wasn't just because I had zero interest in her. I was also working while taking courses online. I didn't have much free time and any free time that I did have, I wanted to spend it with someone I was actually interested in. Not some girl that her only goal in life is to marry someone rich. Even if I was straight, Kayla would not be the woman that I would pick for myself. She was the exact opposite of who I would pick.

"We both have busy lives and our free time doesn't always line up. We still text and speak with each other every day, though."

The conversations were kept very short. I'm not a rude person at all, but Kayla, she was dumb. There really wasn't a nice way to put it.

She was stupid.

An airhead.

Literally nothing inside.

The only thing she wanted to talk about was gossip about her other idiot friends. Something I did not care about. Or she was trying to sext with me, again something I did not care for. Jimmy sending me naked photos, now that I could get into.

Kayla was your typical shallow, self-centered rich girl. She had no problems, she had no responsibilities, and she had no desire to make something of herself. She couldn't understand why my working was important to me. To her, I should have quit and just worked for my father. To land a cushy upper management position and just coast. She considered my working in a diner as a low-life position and it was something she needed to be ashamed of. Point of fact, her friends all think I work for my father already, because God forbid she told them the truth.

"That is not enough. A woman needs more than words on a screen or a phone call. You need to prioritize your future. Kayla is part of that. You need to get your mind focused. You are working at the diner, something that was only supposed to bring you experience, and yet you are treating it like it is your career. The work you do there is pitiful compared to the work you will be doing for the company. It is a waste of time, one I am humoring you on for now, though I will not be doing it for very long. Whatever little rebellion you have going on, I strongly advise you to get it out of your system and do it quickly. I will not allow you to jeopardize my company's future. A company that has been in this family for generations. A company you are set to take over within the next few years."

I had heard this lecture all before, not exactly this version, but the bottom line was all the same. I wasn't living up to his expectations or to the family name. That I needed to get my head out of the clouds and focus on the company and how to make it better for the future. That future included me being forced to marry a woman just so there could be a merger with her family. To my father, it wasn't just my duty to the family but my way of bringing honor to us. It was beyond old fashioned, and this was a lecture I quickly became annoyed with and often tuned him out.

"Plan the proposal."

That had me snapping back into attention. I had clearly missed something, something very important that he had added on this time around.

"Proposal?" I asked, trying to make it seem like I hadn't tuned him out. That wouldn't have gone over well.

"How you propose to a woman matters, Zane. They want to remember it for the rest of their lives. You can't just place a ring box down on a table. A woman of her caliber needs a big gesture for it. Just like the ring matters. You should take your mother this weekend to look at rings."

Okay, now I know my father is certifiable. There was no way in hell he was actually talking about me proposing to Kayla, a woman I had only been dating, and I use that term very lightly, for a few weeks. This was turning out to be a shotgun wedding, only this time around the shotgun would be pointing at me and not the bride. He couldn't seriously believe that after only a few weeks of dating I would propose to her.

"There's no need for that just yet,

Father. We have only been seeing each other for a few weeks, now. I understand that this is important, but it is also important that we develop a relationship to ensure a marriage works. If she is not happy, it would not look good to have her filing for divorce."

I needed to get my father to see logic. If it was his idea for us to wait, then he wouldn't keep bringing it up. He wouldn't start to pressure me into a proposal.

"A woman like her will not wait that long to see a true commitment. You cannot drag your feet for very long or she will grow tired of waiting and find someone else that will give her what she needs. You need to start thinking about the future and how you are going to propose to her."

He wasn't going to let this go, which meant I would have no choice but to appease him. I would have to figure out how to get out of this later.

"Yes, Father. I need to go and pick her up now, though. I don't want to be late."

A simple nod from my father had me instantly moving to the door. It was easier for him to believe I was seeing Kayla. I didn't need to deal with any further questions about where I was going and who I was seeing. Not to mention why I wasn't going to see Kayla. I just wanted to see Jimmy. Seeing him would make this night better.

I quickly got into my car and headed off for the downtown movie theatre. We would be meeting there. As much as I would have loved to pick Jimmy up at his house, I was still nervous with people knowing I was gay. You never know who was going to accidentally let something slip to someone else. I had to be vigilant, especially in the beginning. Once people got used to seeing us around and seeing us as being just two guys who were friends, I could pick him up at his house. I could hang out with him there and no one would think twice about it. The movies would allow us to be close while in the dark. I've taken a few dates to the movies before and it always worked out well. I couldn't wait until I could get Jimmy alone in the dark.

Once I parked, I made my way to the front of the building. Downtown tonight wasn't very busy with it being a Wednesday. With mine and Jimmy's work schedule a Friday or Saturday night date wouldn't work. We would be working while everyone else was enjoying their weekend. It being not that busy would help in our favor in the movies, too. It would give us more privacy, and with more privacy, more fun could be had.

Jimmy was already here, standing out front looking sexy as hell. He wore a black t-shirt with a black denim jacket. His jeans were dark blue and I could see paint splatter on them. His black converse shoes also had paint splatter. Most would find it unattractive, but to me, no one had ever looked sexier.

I can't even begin to explain how badly I want to watch him work. I wanted to watch as his creative juices poured out of him and onto the canvas. And once he was finished, I wanted to strip him of his clothes and lay him down on the tarp. I wanted to create our own masterpiece together.

The rich warm smile he sent my way caused a chain reaction within my body. Electricity ran down my spine that was quickly followed by this heat that exploded in my chest and traveled all the way down to my crotch. This man could make me hard with something as simple as a smile.

"Hey, you made it," I said, and flashed him a warm smile. I wished I could have reached out and kissed him.

"I had to set an alarm so I wouldn't get lost in my art. I always paint when I get home from school," Jimmy said with a small shy smile.

"I would love to watch you paint," I said softly as we made our way toward the cashier. I could see the blush creep over his cheeks out of the corner of my eye and it only made him look sexier. Tonight was going to be so much fun.

Once we had our tickets, we headed inside and grabbed some drinks and popcorn to split. I guided us into the theatre and made sure we sat in the back in one of the darker corners. Most people wouldn't want to sit back here and that was what I was counting on. It would allow us to have some privacy that we would need.

"Interesting seats," Jimmy whispered.

"Trust me, these are perfect," I said with a playful smirk. Jimmy had no idea just what I had in store for him.

"It's not very busy." The slight nervous tone to his voice told me that he was feeling anxious. I was as well, but I always was when I was out in public with another guy. My mind was constantly going over the chances of someone discovering that we were on a date.

"It's Wednesday. I would have been shocked if it was. How was school?" I was hoping the topic of school would be enough to help put his nerves at ease.

"It was good. I was able to get most of my projects done ahead so I don't have to stress too much over them. Danny was pretty upset today."

"Danny?"

"He's my friend that I was telling you about that was kicked out. His older brother, Thad, had to have this big meeting with their parents. Apparently, it did not go well."

"What happened, if you don't mind

my asking."

"His parents wanted Thad to place Danny into a conversion camp. Technically, Thad doesn't have custody of Danny so his parents can still make all the decisions. Thad is trying his best to protect him. It's looking like it's going to get ugly. Danny was talking about Thad having to get a family lawyer and sue for custody," Jimmy said with pain in his voice for his friend.

"Shit, I'm sorry. That really sucks and shouldn't have to be like that. How old are Danny and Thad?"

"Danny is sixteen. He's a year behind me in school. And Thad is nineteen. He works as a mechanic. I don't know where they would get the money for a lawyer, but Danny has two years to go before he's legally an adult. From what I gathered, they don't want to roll the dice with that much time left."

"No, I wouldn't want to wait either. That's insane. Why the push for the conversion camp? Or do they just believe they work?"

Conversion camps weren't unheard of, especially in a small town like this one. Still, most parents didn't jump to it.

"They are very religious. They were always strict with him and Thad growing up. They had to only wear certain clothes, they only ever ate healthy food, they went to church four times a week. They weren't allowed to be alone with a girl, no dating. I mean, insane, controlling, strict. Being gay is completely against their religion and means he would be going to hell. Danny said they had apparently been hoping the phase would be washed out of him by now," Jimmy said as he rolled his eyes.

"And now they want to put him through conversion therapy. What are they going to do?"

Conversion therapy wasn't a route that my parents would take. Only because they wouldn't want to have it out in the open that one of their sons was gay. That didn't change the fact that I was worried about Daryl. He only had a year left, but he would still be expected to live at home until he was twenty-five. My parents had their own beliefs and ways. Keeping us home until we get married to the woman they picked and we received our inheritance was their way of controlling us. If we left, our inheritance would be changed and we would lose everything. I was going to make it, but I had serious doubts about Daryl.

"I don't know. Danny didn't know. I think he is hoping that Thad can convince them to wait it out. I doubt he would be able to afford a lawyer. He works all the time now to pay the bills and to put some money away for Danny's college fund. All they can really do right now is wait and see."

It was clear that Jimmy was worried about his friend. I couldn't blame him. It was a terrible situation for them to be in. Hopefully, it would work out and they would able to avoid having to go through the court system. That could be a lengthy and expensive experience. Mechanics didn't make minimum wage, but they didn't make a huge amount of money, either. With having a two bedroom to pay for, plus trying to save money, there wouldn't be much room for unexpected expenses.

"Hopefully, Thad can come to some sort of an agreement with his parents to put a stop to all of this. I'm sure it'll be okay," I said. I reached over and took his hand in mine as the room got darker for the trailers to begin.

"I hope so," Jimmy easily agreed, flashing me a warm smile.

We turned our attention to the movie. While Jimmy was watching it, I was waiting for the perfect moment to make my move. That moment came roughly twenty minutes later when everyone was invested in the movie.

I moved my left hand over to Jimmy's crotch and started to rub it through his jeans. The second my hand made contact, Jimmy jumped slightly in his seat and I couldn't help the small, soft chuckle that escaped my lips. I looked over at him and I could see the shock and confusion on his face, but I could also see the excitement in his eyes.

"You didn't think we'd just watch the movie did you?" I whispered into his ear, causing him to shiver.

"Someone could see," he countered as I started to unzip his pants.

"They are all watching the movie. The only reason they would look at us is if you make a noise."

I freed Jimmy's cock from his pants and he was already hard. I brushed my lips over his neck, nipping and licking at the sensitive spot below his ear as I started to slowly jerk him off.

Jimmy must have decided that holding the popcorn bucket was too much effort right now, and he placed it down on the seat beside us. What he did next, though, did surprise me. He reached over and started to unzip my own jeans to free my already hard cock.

A quick scan of the room only confirmed what I already knew, everyone was looking at the giant screen. I let out a huff at the contact of Jimmy's warm hand along my hard shaft. He felt amazing. I wished we could have had sex right now, but people would notice that for sure. Handjobs, not so much. Still, what I wouldn't give to be buried deep inside of him again.

It wasn't long before we were both breathing heavy and having to keep our moans and groans internal and not out loud. If we didn't have to worry about the thirty some odd people in the theatre hearing us, these walls would be echoing with our pleasure-filled sounds.

"Zane," Jimmy whispered, and I felt his cock getting harder within my hand.

He was reaching his peak and I was closely following behind him. Normally, I could last a lot longer, but there was something about Jimmy that made me go crazy. Every single touch of his felt amplified by a hundred times.

Jimmy moved and buried his face into my neck as he gave a groan and came hard, his cum quickly spilling down my hand with each pulse. Feeling his cock pulse in my hand, feeling his warm cum spreading over my skin, pushed me over the edge and I had to bite down on my lip to keep what would have been a very loud groan from escaping.

We both fought to catch our breaths as we pulsed in the other's hand. And just like that, all of the nerves and anxiety about tonight were gone.

He was amazing.

We were amazing together.

Jimmy turned his head toward the screen and after a moment he spoke.

"Who's that guy?"

I couldn't help the small chuckle. "I have no idea."

Jimmy laughed as he pulled his hand away from my still hard cock and grabbed us some napkins. We were both a mess, but it was a good mess.

After quickly getting cleaned up and settled back into our pants, we sat back and tried to catch up on the movie. I had no idea what was going with it, but so far it was my new favorite movie.

CHAPTER SEVEN

Jimmy

IT HAS BEEN a month now since Zane and I started dating. Everything had been going amazingly. I had forgotten what it was like to date someone. To have someone in my life that I could talk with and share different personal aspects of my life. I know I can tell my parents anything, just like I could tell my friends anything, but it's different with a boyfriend. Having someone know you on a physical and intimate level brought a stronger connection and it was that connection I'd missed.

I missed the little moments, the kisses goodbye, the quick kiss on the cheek, holding hands, being curled up in his arms while we watched television or lying together in bed. Being with Zane brought a certain feeling to my chest. A warmth I didn't think I needed, but he had proved me wrong. There was something real brewing between us and I wanted to experience more of it.

My parents were in absolute love with him, not that I could blame them. They weren't happy that he was in the closet, but they had to respect it. Their worries were put at ease when they discovered that it would only be short-term. I think to them, though, they were looking at the big picture.

Statistics weren't exactly on our side. Chances were we wouldn't still be together in five years time. I would be going off to College and he was staying here. I understood that the odds were not in our favor, and that was before you factored in our ages.

Still, I wasn't going to let that get to me. I was going to live my life to the fullest and if Zane was standing by my side, then I would be eternally happy. I could hope, though, that it worked out. I could hope we could make it work and last long enough for Zane to be able to come out to his parents.

At the same time, though, I was keeping a piece of my heart safely tucked away behind a cement wall three feet thick. I had learned enough from my past relationships to know that a man in the closet brought pain with him. Brought feelings like you weren't good enough, annoyance, frustration, and impatience.

He had to stay in the closet, and I understood fully, but he was also going to have to understand that I was going to have to keep some level of emotional distance with him. At least, until we'd been dating long enough for me to see how exactly this was going to work.

Sitting down outside at the cafe once again for lunch, I could tell that something seemed to be bothering Zane. He tended to furrow his eyebrows when he was stressing about something. When he had something on his mind he would look down and not really notice anything that was going on around him.

This is where we differed greatly. Me, I'm an open book. If something is bothering me you will be hearing all about it. I never keep things bottled up inside of me. It was bad for my art. Now, yes, there are plenty of times when I paint my emotions and my pain away, but that is to cleanse my mind and soul from it. I have to talk in order to be able to properly paint, to properly draw and release my creative juices.

Zane, though, kept everything under lock and key. It made sense, considering he had to hide the biggest part of himself from the world. Having to keep a secret that personal and enormous took a toll on you. Plus, based on what little he had spoken about his parents, they weren't the 'hug you and make it all better' type. They didn't come across as people who wanted you to spill all of your secrets and emotions out to them. Zane's mom would not be sitting curled up in bed with him with a pint of mint chocolate chip to listen to his boy problems. He was used to going through life keeping things bottled up and going through it all alone.

It was clear even with past boyfriends he didn't open up to them. I wanted Zane to know, to understand, that he could tell me things. That if something was bothering him, I was there for him. That I would be on his side and it wasn't just because we were dating. It was because he clearly needed someone to just be on his side. Right or wrong, he needed a person standing in his corner ready to face the world with him.

"What's on your mind, Z?" I asked, using the nickname for him while we were outside. I was the type of guy that loved pet names. I loved calling my boyfriend 'baby' or 'honey', but we couldn't do that right now. So I call him Z while we are outside around people so he knows that he's special to me.

"Nothing, J," Zane said with a teasing smirk.

A quick roll of my eyes told him I was not impressed with his new nickname. He was still trying to find something that would work for me while we were out in public. That one was a serious no go.

"Never, ever, again."

The rich chuckle that escaped him only warmed my heart. It would have brought flutters to fill my chest if his smile had actually reached his eyes. Something was seriously bothering him and we were not going to enjoy our day together until we cleared it up.

"I'll keep trying, but you're the creative one between us."

"Yes, I am, but I refuse to give myself a nickname. Now, what is bothering you?"

"I said nothing."

"Yeah, tell that to the troubled look on your face or the distant look in your eyes. Something is bothering you. Tell me what it is so we can work it out," I said calmly. I knew this was going to take a wee bit of teeth pulling, but it would be worth the work.

"It's fine, I can work it out myself," Zane said, looking to dismiss the conversation all together.

"I know you are used to handling things on your own. Just like I know it will take you some time to get used to having someone in your life that you can talk to. I am respecting your pace, but every now and then I need to give you a little tiny push up the hill. This is me pushing nicely," I said and flashed him a warm smile.

Zane took a deep breath in and slowly let it out. I had discovered that meant he was debating internally and needed a moment to get his thoughts in order. Needed that minute or two to list the pros and cons before he would make his decision. Hopefully, the pros would be in my favor this time around. The waitress brought our drinks over and we quickly placed our food order. Once we were alone again, Zane spoke.

"My father has been asking me when I am going to propose to Kayla."

That was not what I was expecting to hear. I figured it might have been something to do with his school work or his parents. I didn't expect for it to be about Kayla. I didn't even know they were still seeing each other. I know they had gone on a date before Zane and I kissed. Before we started to see each other, but I figured he was finished with her.

Was he still seeing her while seeing me?

Was I the dirty mistress?

"I didn't know you were still seeing her," I said in a hushed voice, doing my best to keep the pain from my voice. I didn't want him to know that it bothered me that he might be seeing her along with me. It was one thing to be in the closet, but another for me to be just someone else that he was sleeping with. Even if the other person was a woman.

"You are the only person I am with. You are the only person I am seeing. The only person I am spending time with. You are the only person I *want* to spend time with," Zane reassured with a deep strength to his voice that instantly had me feeling better.

"You are the only person I want to spend time with, Z."

It made me feel good to hear him say that. To hear that he was only sleeping with me, only dating me. Still, it brought up more questions about Kayla.

Why would his father be asking when he is going to propose if he wasn't seeing her?

"My father thinks I'm still seeing her. We keep texting, but I keep blowing off her requests for a date. I just tell her I'm working or have to do something for my father. My father, as you know, has basically promised me to her and her to me. I didn't get a say in it, it's all business to him. The sooner we get married, the better it will be for the family company."

The bitter tone to his voice was subtle, but I could easily pick it up. Not that I could blame him. He was basically being forced into an arranged marriage and it wasn't because of his religion, but so his father could make more money and have more prestige. It was despicable in my opinion and no way for a father to be treating his child.

"Have you thought about how you are

going to do this long-term? I mean, Z, you're almost four years away. You can't just keep leading her on, that's not fair to her."

I had never met her and Zane didn't say much. I just knew from what Zane had told me that she was more interested in being a trophy wife than actually working and making something of herself. I couldn't hold that against her, lots of women can be like that if they grow up in a highly wealthy family. How she was brought up or her personality didn't mean she deserved to be lead on. To be thinking that she was going to get married and eventually fall in love with someone only for the other person to hold zero interest in her. That wasn't fair to her at all and she didn't deserve to have that level of pain placed on her.

"I know, I know," Zane said, as he rubbed both hands over his face before he continued. "I'm hoping that maybe she'll be the one to quit. To get tired of me blowing her off. She spends all day long with other rich guys, she's bound to find someone that will give her the attention she needs. I've just been trying to avoid her and hope for the best at this point."

"And I hope for both of your sakes that it works that way. That she finds someone else and her father just wants her to be happy and doesn't care about the merger. But, Z, what if they do care? What if they don't care if she falls in love with someone else?"

I know what I was asking him was a lot and I know it wasn't an easy answer.

The reality was, he didn't have the answers to any of these questions and he was never going to. It was something we would have to wait and see on, that was our only option. The problem was, I hated that we would have to wait. I hated that there wasn't a clear move we could make to put an end to Kayla and their impending engagement.

"I know this puts you in a shitty position, and I can't tell you how sorry I am that I've put you in this position. I wish I had answers for you. I wish I had answers for me, but I just don't right now. It's something I'll have to figure out down the road when a problem presents itself. I would completely understand, though, if you can't do this, if you don't want to do this."

The calm and understanding tone to

his voice told me that he wouldn't hold any of this against me. That we could just go right back to being friends and co-workers. The problem was, I didn't want that. I didn't want to go backward. I wanted to move forward. And in moving forward, I would have to accept a higher level of uncertainty, of the unknown, than I would in a traditional relationship. It was a bigger risk that I was placing myself in, but it was my decision to be here and I wasn't about to change that now.

"I appreciate the out, but I'm not going anywhere. I know this is hard for you, more so than me because you have to deal with it all everyday. You don't get to escape it. I'm not looking for an out. I'm not looking to go back to just being friends. It's early days, I know, but I also know we have something. Being with you feels differently than my previous boyfriends and I know you feel it, too. I believe it's something worth pursuing, so we will face the problems as they come up together. We'll work through them and see what happens."

I wasn't the type of person who needed a plan for everything. I could roll with the punches and just see where the chips would fall. This was a very different situation compared to anything I'd ever been in before, but Zane was worth it. Whatever was going to happen in the future could all be worked out. I was just going to enjoy the ride and enjoy the time I got to spend with him. Hopefully Kayla would just be a blip in the very far distance soon enough.

"Being with you feels special. You feel

special and I don't want to lose that. I'm going to do my best to do right by you while navigating my father's demands. Because what we have *is* different and I want to explore it to the fullest with you. But if there is ever a time, if you reach a point where you can't do this anymore, then I need you to promise me that you'll tell me. I won't be mad. I won't try and convince you to stay. I'll let you go, because I just want you to be happy and I know what I'm asking of you won't be easy and the last thing I want is for you to be miserable."

"I promise."

It was the least I could do for him. This wasn't going to be easy and I was confident there were going to be plenty of times where I was going to be frustrated and wanted to scream at the world. At the same time, though, I also knew there were going to be moments that I would cherish forever. Moments where I felt unbelievable and cared for.

It was those moments I would need to hold on to. Those moments that I would need to remember when times got hard. Those moments would get me and him through this until we reached that finish line. And I wanted to reach that finish line more than anything else. It wasn't just so we could be free to express our feelings in public. It was so Zane would finally be able to be himself. To walk hand in hand without feeling like he had to hide something. For him to just be free to openly show affection toward the man he cared for. He deserved it and I was really hoping I would be around to see it. To watch as he bloomed into his own true self. He was going to be remarkable and, hopefully, together we would be remarkable.

CHAPTER EIGHT

Zane

FIVE MONTHS, IT was crazy to think that we had been together for five months, now. Time had flown by and I am fairly certain there are a lot of people that would think something is wrong with me that I would expect for five months to be a long time, but to me it was.

I hadn't dated someone this long since my very first boyfriend back in high school. Most of the time it was only a friends with benefits situation or a one-night stand at the club. There were no dates, no cuddling, no hand holding, it was just sex and then a see you next time. It was beyond casual and simple. So to me, five months was a huge accomplishment.

Tonight we had gone to the movies, it was our new favorite spot because we could hide in the back and be alone. We tended to now go and watch movies that we didn't care about so we could enjoy the other's body while it was playing.

The past five months, Jimmy had been my salvation. Spending time with him in and outside of work was the only thing that kept me from going insane. I was still dealing with Kayla and all of the drama that came with it. She was upset that we weren't going on dates and that I wouldn't sext with her. There were only so many times I could tell her I was a proper gentleman and preferred to take things slow with her to build a better relationship. She was getting annoyed and both of our families knew it. That was putting more pressure on me from my father, who was all but demanding that I go and buy her an engagement ring. Things were getting intense, to say the least, so any time I got to spend with Jimmy was my saving grace.

Being around him made me feel light, as weird as that sounds, but when I was around him I didn't have to be weighed down by all of the pressure and stress from my daily life. I didn't need to have all of the walls up to protect myself. I could just be me and Jimmy made me feel like being myself was enough.

We had been getting closer over the past five months, spending a lot of time together will do that. I was falling for him. If I was honest with myself, I had already fallen for him. It was so fast, too fast, but it had happened. I hadn't told him yet. I couldn't tell him. It was too soon and I didn't want to scare him away. If there was one thing I couldn't lose, it was him. I had never been in love before; it was all new to me and I wasn't exactly sure how I felt about it.

When I wasn't around him, I was constantly thinking about him, dreaming about him. Sometimes I would get so caught up in my mind that I wouldn't even notice that my parents were speaking with me. I had easily covered it up by lying, saying I was thinking about Kayla or work. When we were together, though, it took all of my strength not to touch him. I wanted to hold his hand, to kiss him, hug him. I wanted to scream from the rooftop that he was my boyfriend. I couldn't do that, though. Not yet.

It was different for me, because before I never cared about any of that. I was perfectly content to play friends and not get personal with them. Jimmy was different. He made me feel things I never expected to ever feel in my life. He made the logical part of my brain shut off when were alone.

"This place is so pretty at night," Jimmy said, snapping me out of my thoughts.

We were currently walking through a park that wasn't too far away from the downtown strip. It was dimly lit with a few light posts scattered around. It wasn't too dark that we couldn't see, but it was dark enough that I could hold his hand without anyone seeing us.

"It's not the only thing that is pretty at night," I said back to him.

It wasn't a line; he was breathtaking in the moonlight. The way the muted light played across his face, and his eyes actually sparkling in the moonlight, he was beautiful, absolutely beautiful.

I stopped and pulled him into my arms. I just couldn't help myself. I knew I shouldn't be doing this, but the need to feel his lips against mine was far too great. I pulled Jimmy in for a kiss and I could feel the shock through his lips, but it only lasted a split second before he was responding and kissing me back.

The world around us completely disappeared. All that was left was Jimmy and his lips, his sweet tasting lips. I had never been a huge fan of kissing, I much preferred to skip that step and go straight to fooling around, but with Jimmy, I could spend all day long kissing him and never get tired of it.

"Well, look at what we have here, boys. We got ourselves some faggots."

The foreign voice instantly had us pulling apart. I quickly looked over Jimmy's shoulder to see eight twenty-something year olds not too far from us. I was so lost in the kiss and what I was feeling that I didn't even hear them coming. I moved so Jimmy was behind me as I spoke.

"We're not looking for trouble. We're just heading home."

I wasn't sure what would happen with them. I hadn't come across something like this before, but I could guess it would only go one of three ways. They left, they stayed and said horrible shit to us, but allowed us to leave, or they attacked us. I was really hoping it wouldn't be option number three. I could fight, but I knew Jimmy couldn't and even if he could, we were still widely outnumbered.

"You should have thought of that before you decided to kiss in public. Ain't nobody wants to see that disgusting shit," the man said, as the other seven started to move around us. It looked like they were going to go with the third option. All I could do now was try and protect Jimmy as best as I could. Maybe if they saw me as the bigger threat they would leave Jimmy alone.

"Then walk away. We're not bothering you," I countered.

I could feel Jimmy shaking slightly behind me. He had yet to say anything and that was a good thing right now. I wanted their attention on me.

"You're bothering us by existing," another man said from behind us.

They were closing in, so I did the only thing I could think of. I moved back toward the one large tree just off to the left of us. I made sure Jimmy was directly behind me so he would have his back to the tree, putting me right in their sights. It wouldn't protect me, but it would protect Jimmy.

"I want you to run toward the street.

Go as fast as you can and don't look back," I softly whispered.

"I can't leave you," Jimmy countered.

"Yes, you can. You have to so you can get help. I mean it, run."

I knew what I was asking him would be hard and that he wouldn't want to do it, but he had to. The only way we were both going to get out of this alive would be if he could get away.

Before any more could be said, the guys were moving on us. I swung out at the first one I could and my fist connected with his jaw, knocking him down. I was hoping if I could hold their attention for a minute or two, then that would give Jimmy enough time to run. I didn't have time to check and see if Jimmy was running or not. I had fists flying at me in all directions. I was trying to keep up, but there were just too many of them. I was being grabbed and thrown around.

By the time I ended up on the ground, I was a good twelve feet away from Jimmy. Jimmy, who hadn't gotten very far from the tree where we started, had five guys on him. He was on the ground trying to protect himself. I could see through the punches and kicks that connected with my body, that they were kicking him repeatedly to his leg.

His eyes were closed and I was praying that he was unconscious and they would leave him alone. A sharp kick to my head sent blackness circling my vision. I couldn't really see, but I could vaguely hear them talking. I could hear their voices and the words, but I couldn't really tell how many were talking or where they were coming from.

"Come on, we don't have to do this. Let's just leave."

"These faggots need to learn a lesson."

"Not like this. We've already given them a beat down, let's get the hell out of here before we get caught."

"Relax, no one is going to come looking for these faggots. Get his pants off."

Hearing those words had me forcing my eyes to focus.

What the hell were they talking about?

Whose pants were they taking off?

I looked around, blinking hard as I felt my body giving in to unconsciousness. I forced myself to stay awake. I had to know what was going on, what was going to happen. To my horror they were removing Jimmy's pants and the ringleader had a small branch in his hand.

Jimmy was completely unconscious; he had no idea what was going on. I was praying that someone would stop them, that someone would see us and save Jimmy from what was about to be done to him. I could just vaguely make out the evil smirk on the ringleader's face as he got down in between Jimmy's legs. I couldn't hold on any longer, though, as the ringleader moved the branch closer to Jimmy, everything went black.

****

Pain, that was the only word for it. Everything hurt, my entire body was screaming out in pain. I had no idea where I was, but the thought of having to open my eyes was unappealing. It hurt to think, I couldn't imagine actually seeing.

I settled for lying there, trying to use my other senses to tell me where I was or what was going on. There was something soft underneath me, a bed it felt like.

Maybe me and Jimmy had made it back to his place, but why would I be in pain?

Why would my head feel like I had a hundred jackhammers going to town inside?

If I was hung over, this was the worst hangover of my life. I couldn't have gotten drunk last night, though, that wouldn't make sense. I was with Jimmy and he's not old enough to drink.

What the hell happened last night?

Okay, focus.

Last night...

What did we do last night?

I got ready to meet up with Jimmy. We were going to the movies and then something, it's that something that I needed to figure out. That something led to whatever this is.

If I could just get my head to stop pounding, I might actually be able to think, to remember. I needed to open my eyes, that would at least tell me whose bed I was in. Maybe Jimmy knew what happened.

Slowly, I forced my eyes to open, I had to know where I was and what happened. I couldn't keep lying here all day or all night. I realized I didn't even know what time it was. I had to blink a few times to get rid of the blurriness that greeted me. Only, when I could see, it didn't ease my confusion at all.

I was in an all white room and the distinct smell of disinfectant told me it was a hospital room. A quick scan told me I was alone, so my parents either hadn't been called or they had and were just not here.

The dim light that made its way through the window told me it was morning. It also told me I had a concussion, if the extreme shot of pain from looking at it was any indication. I'd never had a concussion before, but I had a couple of friends that did from playing sports. They all said the same thing, it was like having a hangover times a hundred. Even your eyeballs hurt and you couldn't always walk a straight line in the early days. I was not looking forward to that. The concussion would also explain the haziness over last night.

Did I crash my car?

Cautiously, I moved the blanket down and saw a hospital gown. I couldn't help but groan at seeing it. I moved slowly, but I could see that my arms were both covered in bruises and my hands were banged up and sore, like I had been in a fight.

Oh shit.

I had been in a fight.

It was as if a switch had been flipped in my mind. Suddenly, the images of last night came pouring back in. We'd been in the park and I couldn't help myself, I had to kiss him. All logic went out the window and the need to feel his skin against mine became all consuming.

Those few moments of kissing, though, brought us both a world of pain.

Eight guys jumped us.

Jimmy, I had to get to Jimmy. I had to know if he was okay. What they did to him... *Oh fuck*, what they did to him. I have to see him. I need to talk to him.

Pushing through the pain, I forced my body to sit up. I couldn't suppress the groan that escaped from the pain shooting all across my ribs, stealing my breath. I had no idea if any were broken, but they sure as shit felt like they were.

None of it mattered, though.

I had to get to Jimmy.

I could see a small black duffle bag on the one chair, so someone had been by since last night and was kind enough to bring me a change of clothes. Whoever it was, I loved them immensely right now.

Bit by bit, I managed to stand up. I had to hold onto the bed as the entire room spun on me. Still, I managed to get to the chair and pull out some sweatpants, a long sleeved shirt, and some socks. My shoes were on the floor underneath the chair and I was not looking forward to trying to get them on. I would do it, though. Any pain I felt would be nothing compared to the pain Jimmy was in.

If anyone asked how long it took me to get dressed, I would be embarrassed to answer. I would also deny the fact that getting my shirt on almost made me curl up into a ball and cry, but I was dressed.

Making sure I held onto the walls, I made my way out of the room and slowly made my way down the hallway. I had no idea where Jimmy was, but if I could find a nurses' desk or something, I could ask where he was and find his room.

After finding a nurses' desk and going through the annoying conversation about how I was supposed to be in bed, she finally told me what floor and room Jimmy was in. He was two floors up from me in the ICU wing, something that had my heart plummeting into my stomach. She couldn't tell me anything about his condition because I wasn't family, but I was hoping his parents would be up there. They were good people. They wouldn't leave his side like my parents apparently had. I would have to face that tidal wave of emotions later.

Right now, the only thing that mattered was Jimmy.

SHATTERED

After taking the elevator up and heading down the hallway, I was finally standing out front of Jimmy's room. Just like I thought, his parents were there, sitting beside his bed, ready for whenever he woke up or needed something.

My gaze only lingered on them for a moment, before they focused on the only person in that room that mattered to me. Seeing Jimmy did nothing to ease my fears. I had no idea what any of the machines did, but he wasn't intubated so he was breathing on his own. I wasn't certain, but the heart monitor looked okay, the beats looked good, but what the hell did I know? I barely passed biology. I knew nothing about any of this stuff.

The injuries on Jimmy that I could

see only made me feel worse. His right eye was swollen shut and he was covered in bruises; I could see them even from where I was standing. He also had a black leg brace on his right leg from his thigh down to his knee. It must have been broken or sprained. Based on the bruises and the swollen eye, he must have had a concussion as well.

What worried me and confused me would be why he was up here and I wasn't. I knew that Jimmy would have an additional injury from the assault, but why would he need to be in the ICU? Something else had to be wrong, something that I wasn't seeing.

I should be going in there. I should be sitting next to his bed and holding his hand, but I couldn't bring myself to open the door.

SHATTERED

This was my fault.

I should have prevented this.

I should have protected him.

I should never have lost control and kissed him. If I hadn't, then they wouldn't have known that we were gay and none of this would have happened.

I knew logically it wasn't my fault. That they were homophobes and I wasn't responsible for their actions, but I didn't feel that way right now. There was no logic running through my mind at the moment, only deep guilt that brought tears to my eyes.

It was that moment that his parents turned to look at the door. Maybe they sensed my presence. They were both getting to their feet and coming out. I was prepared for them to tell me to leave, to get the hell away from their son.

It would destroy me to do it, but I would out of respect for them. I just needed to know how bad it was and to let them know how sorry I was.

"Zane. Sweetie, you should be in bed. You have a serious concussion," Jimmy's mother said in a soothing voice that only made the tears start to flow.

"I'm sorry. I'm so sorry. I tried to get them away from him. There were too many."

Jimmy's mother instantly pulled me into her arms as she spoke. "No. Oh, Sweetie, no. You did nothing wrong. This is not your fault. None of this is your fault. They were in the wrong. He's going to be okay. You both are going to be okay."

Hearing that Jimmy would recover from his injuries made the dam break inside of me. I held on to his mother for dear life as the sobs shook my entire body. I felt a firm hand on my shoulder from his father, providing me with what comfort he could. I wasn't sure how long we all stood there as I let the pain out before I was pulling back. I quickly wiped away the tears from my cheeks as I cleared my throat so I could speak.

"How bad are his injuries?"

"He has a concussion, bruising all over his torso and arms, his eye is still swollen, but it was only just last night the attack happened. The doctor said it would go back to normal in a week or so. He needed to have surgery on his right thigh, there was blunt force trauma and damage done to the nerves. He needed to have a graft made in order to save the function of his leg. It was successful, but he will need to go through physical therapy to relearn how to walk with that leg. He'll be on crutches for a few months, at the least. He needed stitches from the assault, but the doctor assured us that he would make a full recovery and there won't be any permanent damage. With his concussion, there's a good chance he won't remember any of the attack, which will be a blessing. You, though, you have a concussion and two very bruised ribs and should be in bed resting still."

"I'm fine. I should have done more. I should have done something. I love him. I love him and I couldn't protect him from this." Tears welled up in my eyes all over again and I fought to hold them back from spilling over.

"What did you just say?"

The sound of my father's voice had me snapping my head to the right. The room spun for a moment at the sudden movement and I had to close my eyes for a second to prevent myself from falling over. When I opened them, I saw my father standing there with a very pissed off look on his face. With him, though, was my mother, looking indifferent as always, and Daryl.

The shocked look on Daryl's face told me that they had heard everything I just said. He wasn't expecting me to say that I was in love with another man. The shock was justified. I had never confided in him that I was gay, not even after he admitted it to me. It was just further proof that my kid brother was braver than me.

"Father, what are you doing up here?"

I needed to buy some time. I needed to figure out what I wanted. I really only had two options, deny my love and explain it away as something else. Or I could admit to being gay. I wasn't sure which road I was going to take yet.

"We went to your room and a nurse said you were up here looking to see the other boy. Now, what the hell game are you playing at here, Boy? You are not in love with that faggot. Tell me I did not just hear you say you were."

There was a sharp edge to my father's tone and for the first time in my life, I wondered if he would actually snap and attack me. He had always kept himself composed. Yes, there were times he teetered on the edge, but he never went over. Today, though, he might actually tumble off that edge.

This was the moment where my life could either change, or I would continue to be stuck in limbo, waiting out my prison sentence before finally having my freedom. The problem was, I don't know if I wanted to wait. I was standing here at a parole hearing and the judge was telling me to just admit it and I could go free right this very second.

Was staying in prison really worth my inheritance?

Was the money truly worth having to continue on lying and denying a huge part of who I am?

I couldn't help but look over at Daryl and see what his reaction to all of this was. His eyes told me everything I needed to know, they always did. He was completely expecting me to deny it, to lie and keep on pretending. Underneath that, though, there was hope. Hope that I would stand up to our father, not just for myself, but for the both of us.

It was at this moment that I knew I couldn't lie. I couldn't do that to myself, but more importantly, I couldn't do that to Daryl.

"I don't know what you heard, Father, so allow me to clarify. I am madly in love with Jimmy. I have been with him for months, now. Just like I have been with other guys since I was a teenager. I'm gay, whether you like it or not, and I am done denying who I am just to make you feel more comfortable."

Previously, I would have cringed at the very idea of ever telling my parents I was gay. I thought it would leave me feeling empty and nervous, ashamed even. But it didn't.

SHATTERED

There was this joy that flooded my chest. There was no shame, no guilt, nothing but pure joy and the sweet breath of freedom. This feeling, it was worth it all. It was worth every bruise on my body. Every dollar that he would steal from me. It was all worth it just to finally be free from him.

"You are a disgrace to this family. You have brought disgrace to my name. If you want to be a fag, fine, but you are not welcome in my home. You are not welcome in this family. You're dead to us," Father said with a deadly calm that I knew did nothing to showcase how furious he truly was. If we were at home, things would have been broken, but he wasn't about to put on a show here in the public.

Him and my mother quickly turned

and started to head off. I was expecting for Daryl to follow them, but instead he ran toward me and wrapped his arms around me. I held in the groan of pain; I didn't want him to feel bad for hurting me. He clearly needed the comfort and I was happy to give it. I wrapped my arms tightly around him as I whispered into his ear.

"It'll be okay. I'll be okay, I promise. You just stay quiet and out of his way for a little bit. Don't tell him. We can do that together when you're eighteen and free to make your own decisions. I'll figure something out for you, I promise, Squirt."

He just gave a nod against my chest before he spoke. "I love you, Z."

"I love you, too. Now go on, before he comes back looking for you."

I didn't want to send him away, especially with our father, but I couldn't do anything just yet. We had to wait until Daryl was legally an adult before we could get him away.

Daryl pulled back and quickly took off down the hallway to catch up.

Once they were gone, the adrenaline began to wear off and I was feeling it in my body as weakness set in hard and fast. I moved back and used the wall to help support my weight.

Jimmy's father placed a strong hold on my arm to help steady me.

"I'm okay. Sorry you had to experience that." This would have been the first time Jimmy's parents met mine and that didn't exactly go the traditional route.

"You don't have to apologize for them.

They are the ones that are ass backward here. I'm very proud of you, though. What you did was very brave and you should be proud of yourself for finally standing up to them. For accepting who you are and knowing that there is nothing wrong with you," Jimmy's father said with a deep truth to his voice.

His words instantly soothed my fears and I could see, now, how Jimmy was so comfortable and confident with himself. He had two amazing parents that got him there.

"Thank you."

Though the simple words didn't seem like enough, it was all I had. I didn't know what else to say other than that. Maybe if I hadn't been concussed and flooded with all sorts of different emotions right now, I would be able to find the words. Thankfully, they both seemed to understand how deeply I meant them.

"Come on, you need to be in bed. I know you want to see him, but he just came out of surgery not even two hours ago. The doctor said he's going to be out for at least eight hours. He's stable, but he's sleeping right now. There isn't anything we can do for him right now but sit in very uncomfortable plastic chairs. Something your body does not need to experience, especially in your current state. Let's get you back into bed. I am sure now that you are awake deputies will be coming to speak with you about the attack. We can work everything else out tomorrow," Jimmy's mother said warmly, as she placed her hand on my arm and started to guide me back toward the elevator.

I didn't want to leave. I wanted to sit next to Jimmy, even if that was in an uncomfortable plastic hospital chair. I wanted to be able to see him and be there for when he opened his eyes. The problem was, Jimmy's mother was right. There wasn't anything I could do right now and my body was already screaming for sleep.

I was so tired and dizzy that if she wasn't holding my arm, I was sure I would be on the floor. I didn't even think about deputies or the sheriff coming down to speak with me. This whole situation could turn into a nightmare if the men were never caught or if anyone within the Sheriff's department were homophobes. With the likelihood of only myself being able to remember, it would fall onto my shoulders to testify and do whatever I needed to do to ensure Jimmy got justice.

And I would do it.

I couldn't help him right now, but I could by being ready to make my statement. I owed it to the man that I loved and I was not about to let him down. Not again.

CHAPTER NINE

Jimmy

WAKING UP IN the hospital for a second time was a lot smoother than the first.

When I first woke up, it was to discover my body in a world of pain and I had no idea why my natural instinct was to cry. Thankfully, my parents were both with me and they quickly soothed and calmed me down.

I was still in a lot of pain, but at least this time I knew why and where I was. It was a surreal experience to know that I was attacked, assaulted, but to have zero memories of it all.

It didn't feel real, like it was someone else's story and I was just playing a role. There should have been emotions attached to it. I should have felt violated and upset, and to a degree I did, but without the physical memories it was as if there was this disconnect within me. It left me feeling weird, like I was supposed to be a certain way. What I was, though, was grateful.

I didn't want those memories. I didn't want to wake up and remember everything with perfect clarity. I wanted to stay in my blissfully ignorant bubble and never leave and I didn't think people would blame me.

After all, who would want those memories by choice?

Forcing my eyes to finally open, I was surprised not to see my parents right next to my bed. I was very surprised and happy to see Zane's head next to me. He slept in a hospital chair and bent over onto the bed. It did not look comfortable at all. I didn't want to wake him just yet, though. I used this time to look him over for myself.

The last time I woke up, I wanted to see him, but when my mom had gone to get him he was asleep. She said he desperately needed the rest and she would go back and check on him later to see if he was awake. They had told me he was injured from the attack, had a concussion like me, but he also had two badly bruised ribs and was covered in bruises. Looking at him now, I could see all of the bruises that were all over his arms and his face. He should still be in bed.

The one thing my parents did tell me, Zane wasn't as lucky as me in the forgetting department. He remembered it all and it broke my heart for him. I was the lucky one, in my opinion. I was more physically injured, yes, but I would heal.

Zane would have to heal with all of the memories from that night. He would always remember it. He would have to do a different type of healing, one that didn't have a set number of days that you could count down from.

I reached over and ran my fingers through his hair. It only took a moment before Zane took a deep breath in and his eyes fluttered open. It only took him a moment before his mind clicked in and then he was sitting up as he spoke.

"Hey, you're awake. How are you feeling? Do you need me to get the nurse?"

His concern and worry for me was sweet, but I didn't want him to worry over me. My body would heal and, eventually, I would put all of this behind me. I wasn't looking forward to the recovery time or with having to learn how to walk again with my right leg. I was also worried about school. I couldn't lose this semester, everything was riding on me graduating. Zane had his own healing he needed to do, and he wouldn't be doing it if he was too busy being focused on me.

"I'm okay. I have pain meds, so that

helps with the bulk of the pain. How are you? You should be in bed still, Baby."

Zane grabbed my hand with his while his other moved over to run his fingers through my hair. "There isn't anywhere else I would rather be right now. I'll be fine. I just have to take it easy. I'm so sorry."

"Don't. I don't remember what happened, but I know without a doubt it is not your fault. The guys that attacked us are assholes. Have the police come by?"

I wouldn't really be able to give them much, but I knew they were hoping to speak with me in a few days. The doctor said if my memory came back, it would be within the next week. If I didn't get it back by then, I was never going to. I was torn between hoping it didn't and hoping it did. I didn't want it back. I wanted to save myself from that level of pain. At the same time, it wasn't fair that only Zane remembered. If the guys were arrested, it would rest solely on his shoulders to get us justice and that was a lot of weight for one person to carry. At least if I remembered, we could both carry that weight.

"Real early this morning. I already spoke to them and gave them my statement. They were going to look into it and see if they could find them. The doctor said you could leave in a week and then you'll start physical therapy a month from now. Your parents went to get something to eat and shower. They've been here for the past two days."

"Good, that's good. They need to take care of themselves. They get so worried about me that they forget to eat and sleep. I don't want them to get sick. What about your parents? Have they come by to see you?"

I wasn't really sure how it would work for Zane. He wasn't eighteen like I was, he was twenty-one, so it would make sense for his parents to not sit by his bedside all day and night long. Though, my parents still would no matter how old I was. Zane's parents, though, they were cut from a different cloth to mine. The hurt that spread throughout his eyes told me that something happened.

"What is it? What happened?" I asked gently. I knew you couldn't push with Zane or he would shut down, but we had made a lot of progress within the past five months. Zane was opening up to me easier now and I was hoping that would continue.

"They came by yesterday not long after I woke up. They found me up here talking with your parents and they overheard me saying that we were together. My Father was pissed and started to demand that I say it was a lie. I know I could have lied, but I just didn't want to anymore. I thought I could make it until I was twenty-five, but there is a difference in not admitting it and lying about it. I could go the next five years not admitting it, hiding it, but I couldn't lie about it. He was furious. He disowned me and kicked me out before they stormed off."

Unbelievable.

I could understand that some parents, especially fathers, may have an issue with their son being gay. I mean, I didn't understand it, but I could wrap my head around the concept. But to disown him after he had been attacked, after he could have been killed? It was disgusting. There was no excuse for it. Even if you don't agree with your son's sexuality, he's still your son.

How could they stand there in a hospital and see him injured and then kick him out?

"I'm so sorry. He had no right to do that to you. What happens now?"

"Daryl, he was able to pack up some of my stuff for me before my father got to my room. He's got it in his room right now, until I'm ready to grab it. Your parents have offered for me to stay with you guys until I can get an apartment. If you would be okay with that."

The uncertainty in his voice cut me

deep. He shouldn't feel uncertain about our relationship and I could tell he was feeling a bit off with everything that had happened. It was natural, given the events in the past forty-eight hours.

"I would love for you to stay with us."

Zane being with us was exactly what he needed. To be able to just be himself and be around people who accepted him. I thought it would really help him start to accept and embrace this new path he was on. He didn't have to hide anymore, he could just be himself and proud of who he was.

"It's just temporary. I've already called the diner so I can get more hours next week. I'll work and save up so I can get my own place. Find a two bedroom so Daryl can stay with me once he's eighteen, if he wants. I'll be there, though, so I can help you with your PT and healing.”

It was going to be nice having Zane around the house. Being able to sleep in his arms, getting to wake up next to him. It was going to be exactly what I needed to heal from this attack. Even if it was just temporary, I think it would be really good for us. Give us the chance to just be ourselves in and out of the house, allow our connection to grow. We could heal and recover together and hopefully come out of this stronger than ever.

“Come here. You're too sore to be sitting in that chair all day. I got plenty of room for two,” I said with a warm smile as I wiggled over further.

“You sure? I don’t want to hurt you.”

“You won’t. Come on, you need sleep

and to rest your ribs."

Zane gave in very easily. I had a feeling he would. He made his way onto the bed with me and lay down with a bit of a groan. He was in a lot more pain than he was letting on with me. I was annoyed, but I couldn't hold it against him. He was used to having to always be the strong one. It was going to take him some time to get used to being vulnerable with me. We would get there, though.

Together, we would get through this and, no matter what, I would be there for Zane.

CHAPTER TEN

Zane

THIRTY DAYS HAD never felt so long and gone by so fast at the same time before. The past month had been filled with pain and drama. The pain part was on both me and Jimmy, though he was in a lot more of it then I was.

My concussion and ribs had improved quite a bit before Jimmy was even able to leave the hospital. Still, for the first week that we were at the house, I was pretty useless.

Jimmy was in a lot of pain, mostly from his leg. The doctor had given him some prescription pain pills, but he didn't like taking them. I couldn't blame him, I was the same way.

For Jimmy, they made his mind cloudy and he wasn't able to be as creative as he was used to being. It blocked him from being able to express himself properly on paper. He spent most of his time in bed resting with a sketchbook in his lap and charcoal over his hands. Watching him sketch had actually been some of the best moments within the past month for me. There was a deep peace that took a hold of his entire body when he was drawing. He was gorgeous and I couldn't wait until I could sit back and watch him paint.

Unfortunately, the drama within the past thirty days was all on me. Jimmy and his parents were really good about it all. They had opened their home up to me and even allowed me to sleep in the same bed as their son. They helped me when I was too dizzy or in pain to do much. They were remarkable human beings and proof that nurture really did outweigh nature.

Three weeks ago, before Jimmy was cleared to leave the hospital his father had driven me to my parents' house. I wasn't cleared to drive yet and I needed to get my things that Daryl had managed to save. I thought we were in the clear, but we were only there for two minutes when the sheriff's department had shown up. My father had called them and reported trespassers on his property.

Thankfully, Jimmy's father had been calm enough to explain that I had been kicked out and was just looking to gather my property. The deputy had been very kind and escorted me inside so I could collect whatever was left in my room. There wasn't really anything left that wasn't destroyed. My father's rage had clearly exploded within the room.

After gathering my bags and saying goodbye to Daryl, we were out of there. It was only a week later when the letter came for me in the mail from a lawyer. I still have no idea how my father discovered where I was staying, but he did. I was expecting the letter from the lawyer, but it still hurt to receive it. My inheritance had been revoked and was being allocated to Daryl. I was happy for him, but I also seriously doubted that he would ever see any of his inheritance, either. I couldn't imagine he would be able to hold off until he was twenty-five with them.

My boss had been really great, he was able to give me extra shifts in the week and he had me on the call list if someone had to cancel their shift. It wasn't amazing money, but I was making a bit more than minimum wage. It was enough that it allowed me to keep doing my online program and to save up.

I had offered to pay rent to Jimmy's parents, but they completely refused it. Told me to save it so I can get my own apartment for me and Daryl. I was looking at two bedrooms, but so far I hadn't found one. I was hoping soon one would pop up and I would be able to secure it. It was just a matter of time, now. I didn't have to hide my schooling anymore, so I was spending most of my free time completing my courses so I could start working toward a better job. I was still going to work on the resort, but it would be a bit of a larger process now. That was okay. I wasn't about to let my dream go, not for anyone.

I hadn't spoken to my parents in the past month, but Daryl and me had been texting each other and even calling. I'd made it a habit of texting him everyday so he knew that I was okay and that he wasn't alone. I didn't want him to feel like he had to face the hurricane that was our father without help. Things at the house were getting intense and I hated that Daryl had to be there on his own with all of this. He would be eighteen in less than a year and then he would be free to move out and live the life that he wanted. I was going to be ready for him.

"Do you think it's going to hurt a lot?"

Jimmy's voice snapped me back into the present. We were currently heading back to the hospital so he could attend his first physical therapy session. His parents had to work today and they weren't too happy that they wouldn't be there for it. I was, however, able to take the day off so I could be there for Jimmy. There was no way in hell I was letting him go through this alone.

"I don't know, Babe. Everything I've read said it can be pretty painful the first few times as your nerves get used to working again. This is only your first session, so you might not be doing too much that would cause any pain. No matter what, though, we'll get through it together," I promised with a warm smile as we pulled into the parking lot.

It was natural for him to be worried. Hell, I was worried and I wasn't the one injured. I had done extensive research into physical therapy and it all depended on the type of injury you had. Learning to walk was a process. At first, you learned how to stand up without having to hold onto the bars, then you worked on taking steps, and eventually, walking without support.

Jimmy would be able to switch the crutches for a cane once he was able to hold his weight and walk. Recovery time varied from a couple of months to a year or more.

"I just want to be able to walk for graduation."

I knew that was very important to him. I couldn't blame him. He was so close to graduating high school, it was only natural that he wanted to be able to walk across that stage like everyone else. I was determined to help him achieve that goal.

"You will. You can do anything. This is going to be a breeze for you and that determination of yours," I offered flashing him a warm smile.

It had the reaction I was hoping for. Gone was the doubt and in its place was my Jimmy, confident and ready for a fight.

We got out and we made our way through the hospital to the physical therapy wing. I walked slow, allowing Jimmy to set the pace. He was still a bit awkward with the crutches, but he was getting a lot better at it. I was surprised to see that there were no other patients there, but it was also nice that we could just be ourselves and Jimmy could focus on what he needed to do without feeling like others were watching.

"You must be Jimmy. I'm Sarah and I'll be your physical therapist," Sarah greeted us both with a warm smile, her eyes crinkling at the corners.

"Hi, this is my friend Zane."

"I'm his boyfriend, actually," I instantly corrected.

I had never truly said it out loud to someone like this before and I had to admit, it felt amazing. Jimmy gave me a big, proud smile, and I could tell he was very happy to hear me say that I was his boyfriend. I was enjoying it, too, and I knew that I would be saying it many, many times.

"It's great that you can be here, the first session can be hard on the patient," Sarah said with understanding.

"How does it work?" Jimmy asked.

"Well, today we are going to get you up on the bars and you are going to work on putting weight onto your leg. The first step to walking is standing. Much like when you were an infant, you had to learn how to stand up before your first step. All we are doing is strengthening your muscles and getting your nerves used to working again," Sarah easily explained.

"You ready, Babe?" I asked, knowing that Jimmy had to be the one to make the decision to get started. It was his body and he would be the one going through the pain.

"As I'll ever be," Jimmy said, shrugging and making it clear he was completely unsure about this. He was nervous again now that we were actually here, but he would be okay. I was going to make sure of that.

"So, we are going to be over here," Sarah said as she led us over to the parallel bars. "You are going to grab each bar and stand with your left leg holding your weight. Then you are going to slowly put some weight onto your right leg. Now, this is going to hurt, I'm not going to lie or sugarcoat it. The first time you do it, it's going to hurt, but it will get better as your body gets used to the movement again. Before you know it, standing won't hurt. Then, when we move on to walking, the process will start all over again. I need two things from you."

"Don't cry?" Jimmy said, trying to joke to ease the mood.

Sarah gave us both a friendly smile. "You can cry all you want. Believe me you will not be the first. I've had patients that have cried, screamed, and even swore. You name it, they've done it. The two things I need from you are honesty and faith. I need you to be honest with me when the pain gets too bad so we can take a break. There is pain and pushing through it, and then there is pain that could cause damage and push your recovery back. As determined to get better as you are, you can't let that determination add months onto your recovery. And faith. Faith that the system that I am going to do with you is going to work. If you give me those two things, we can get you walking within four months, assuming you do your exercises at home and give your leg proper rest. We got a deal?"

"If you can get me walking that fast, I'll do whatever you want me to do," Jimmy easily agreed.

I was surprised that Jimmy's leg could be better within four months. That was a huge deal to both of us. It also gave Jimmy something to fight for. The possibility that he could be walking across the stage at graduation was all he needed to hear to put a fire inside of him.

"Perfect. Grab onto the bars and Zane, if you could stand behind him just in case his leg gives out that would be great," Sarah said as she took Jimmy's crutches.

We both moved into place and I put my hands on his hips, ready to hold him up should I have to. I gave him a quick kiss on the cheek before I spoke. "You got this, Babe."

We both turned our attention to Sarah as, together, we started to get Jimmy on the road to walking.

***

I helped to get Jimmy up the stairs to his bedroom. He was pretty sore still from his first session, but I knew from the research I did that his leg would be pretty sore after his physical therapy for a little while yet. The nerves had to get used to working again and that could send a pretty strong pain wave throughout his leg.

His parents were still at work, so we had the afternoon to ourselves.

Jimmy placed his crutches down by the door. He was able to hop around a bit so he wouldn't have to use the crutches all day long. The second I closed the door, he was on me, though. My back hit the door and Jimmy's lips were on mine. I easily kissed him back, but once I felt his hands going to my pants, I placed my hands on his arms gently and pulled him back, breaking the kiss.

"What the hell is wrong? Do you not want me anymore?" Jimmy asked, pissed off, but I could also hear the hurt tone to his voice.

"That's not it at all, Babe." I knew this

conversation was going to happen eventually, but I was hoping it would have been a bit longer. I wasn't fully prepared for this discussion.

"Then what is it? In the past month you have barely even kissed me. So if you still want me, then what is it?"

I knew he had been feeling frustrated and annoyed with me. He wanted to be close, to be intimate with me, but I kept pulling back. It wasn't because of him, it was me probably over thinking things, but I couldn't help it. I didn't realize what it could be doing to him, though, what he could be taking it as.

"I don't want to hurt you," I softly admitted.

He didn't remember and I was happy about that, but he was still assaulted and the very last thing I wanted was to hurt him. Or god forbid, he did remember while we were in the middle of it. I couldn't hurt him like that.

"The doctor cleared me. He said I was completely healed from the assault. I'm not in pain or anything. Nothing you do to me will hurt me. What hurts me is being pushed away every time I try to touch you. When I try to be intimate with you. It makes me feel like you're not attracted to me after the attack. That you don't want me anymore. That hurts me."

"I do want you. And you will always be the most beautiful man I have ever seen. I always want you, it's why I've been pushing you away. Because if we get started, I won't be able to stop and I don't want to hurt you in any way."

Jimmy moved and he placed his

hands on my hips as he spoke. "And I appreciate that, but I want you. I want to feel your hands on my body again. I want you to make me yours." Jimmy moved closer until our lips were just a breath away from the others. "Make me yours, Zane."

I couldn't deny him. Everything in my body wanted him, wanted to feel his skin underneath mine. I closed the distance between us and devoured his mouth. I would never get tired of kissing him. The sweet taste that flooded my mouth when our tongues danced only fueled the fire within me. I was making him mine again today, but this time we would do it differently. I pulled back when the need for air became too much and spoke.

"We'll take it slow this time. I plan on savoring every single second of it."

The arousal and excitement in his eyes told me exactly how badly he wanted this. Today we were taking back the last piece of us that had been taken from us and it was going to be magical.

CHAPTER ELEVEN

Jimmy

FINALLY, WE WERE finally going to have sex again. I knew it'd only been a month since the last time we had sex, but it felt like years to me. It was insane, because before Zane, I could go years without the need for sex. I could easily focus my attention on school or my art. Sex wasn't that high on my priority list.

Yet, with Zane, it felt like I couldn't breathe if he wasn't touching me. The need for his body was overwhelming and to have gone the past month without it, it hurt worse than any of my bruises. I didn't remember the attack. I had been told about it from the doctor, but I didn't have those memories. The doctor's words felt as if he was telling me a story about someone else, there wasn't this deep personal connection that I had.

Still, I knew Zane had that connection. He saw it. He didn't get to have the relief of not being conscious like I had. He didn't get the lucky break of not remembering that night like I do. Even though I had to heal physically from the assault, Zane had to heal emotionally and mentally from it.

I was trying to respect his pace,

respect his need to go slow, but it had been hard. It was hard seeing him pull away from me. It was hard to feel him kiss me on the cheek and not my lips. It was hard to know that there was a possibility that Zane didn't want me like that anymore. That he saw me as this broken and damaged man, now. After a month of healing, of distance, I couldn't do it anymore. If we were never going to be able to move past what happened to me, then I needed to know. I couldn't keep giving my heart to him. If this was the end, then I needed to know.

It was a huge weight off my shoulders to hear that Zane still wanted me. That he was still attracted to me and was just afraid to hurt me. It was sweet, but I didn't want him to be sweet right now. I wanted to feel his hands on my body again. I wanted to feel him inside of me, claiming me as his own.

Zane moved his hand over to my cheek and to the back of my neck as he spoke, "Tell me if you need me to stop."

"Don't ever stop," I easily said back.

Zane gave me a small smirk before he pulled me to him, closing the gap between us. The second his lips touched mine, it was fire all over again. The way this man could kiss always stole my breath. It made my knees go weak and everything inside of me was screaming for more.

My hands were instantly going to his shirt as he went to mine. We pulled apart for a second so we could remove the pesky material blocking us from the other's skin.

The second our shirts were removed,

tossed recklessly to the floor, our lips were back on the other as we began to explore the other's body. I was never going to get tired of the feel of his muscles underneath my fingertips.

Zane moved his hands down to my ass and he lifted me up. I instantly had my legs wrapped around his hips as he moved us over to the bed. He gently placed me down on it before he covered me with his body. With a firm grip on my ass we rubbed our cocks together, moaning at the pleasure the friction brought us.

It wasn't enough, though. I needed more.

I quickly moved my hands down to the front of his jeans, fumbling with the button and zipper in my haste. Zane clearly felt my urgency as he quickly pushed down my sweats. I kicked them off as Zane stood for a second to remove his jeans and boxers the rest of the way.

I sat up and instantly ran my tongue along the tip of his hard dick. I was rewarded by a surprised hiss of pleasure from him. If there was one thing that I had truly missed within the past month, it was the feel of Zane's dick along my tongue, inside of me. He tasted so sweet and I could never get enough.

I ran my tongue along his long shaft before I worked his dick into my mouth, taking him all the way down to the base. The feel of Zane's hand in my hair caused me to moan, sending vibrations down his dick.

"Oh fuck, Babe," Zane moaned breathly.

It had only been a month since we

had done anything, but I knew Zane was just as pent up as I was. When you go from nothing, to having sex almost every day, and then back to nothing, it was hard to get used to it. You had all of this energy and need just bottled up inside of you and I knew we were both going to explode soon. The first time was going to be fast, but we had the whole afternoon alone to enjoy the other's body. Zane proved my point when he pulled my head back after a moment.

"I'm too close. I want to be buried inside of you when I come."

I wanted that, too, but I also had this uncontrollable desire for something more, as well. I wanted to feel him pulsing inside of me, but I also wanted to feel it without a barrier up between us.

I had no idea how Zane felt about it, but it couldn't hurt to ask, right?

"I don't know if you've ever done it or want to, but I'm clean."

"I've never done it before, but I'm clean, too." I was relieved that Zane understood what I was talking about. "Are you sure?"

"I want to feel you, I want you to claim me as yours. But if you don't want to—"

"I want to more than anything," Zane said, cutting me off.

Zane's body was once again covering mine as we moved back further on the bed. He reached over and grabbed the lube from my bedside dresser before he started to kiss his way down my body.

I knew what was coming so I easily laid back and allowed him to worship me. The second I felt the heat of his mouth around my dick, I let loose a deep, throaty moan. I simply couldn't help it and it slipped from my lips. In the past month, I hadn't even touched myself. I was wound up tight and Zane knew how to loosen every single knot within me. He worked my dick like a pro as he started to stretch my ass. He took it slow, making sure he didn't cause any pain. I knew there wouldn't be, but it warmed my heart to know that he was still being careful, even with his own need increasing.

"Baby," I whispered. I was right on the edge; he was keeping me there with his talented mouth and fingers. The need to come was so strong, but I couldn't fall off the cliff yet. I needed just a bit more friction, but he was purposely missing my sweet spot.

I whined when he pulled his mouth and his fingers back. The warm chuckle he gave me did nothing for my annoyance.

"I want to be buried inside of you when you come," Zane said as he kissed my neck, my shoulders, nibbled on my earlobe.

He moved my right leg carefully, spreading my legs so I would be wider for him. He then grabbed the lube and slicked himself up. I couldn't help the butterflies that filled my stomach, only they weren't from nerves, but excitement.

I had always wondered what it would feel like to have sex bareback, but I never actually thought I would do it. That I would find someone that I trusted to this level. It warmed my heart to know that Zane trusted me with this as well. It would be a first for the both of us and it was romantic that we could share it together.

Zane leaned down and gave me a slow and sensual kiss. I was so lost in the feeling of his lips against my own that I almost missed the feel of his tip breaching my hole. There was a slight sting, but that was always expected and I knew soon enough he was going to have my eyes rolling into the back of my head from the pleasure he could bring me.

We continued to battle each other with our tongues as Zane pushed deeper and deeper inside of me. I didn't really think there would be much difference in the feel of it, but I was wrong. It felt amazing to be feeling Zane's actual skin inside of me. There was a warmth to it that a condom never brought.

I could tell that Zane was feeling it, too. Every time he moved forward he moaned into my mouth. When he was finally down to his base, he pulled back from the kiss, breathing heavy.

"Fuck, you feel so good, so warm." Zane groaned, his cock pulsing inside of me as he fought to get control of his need to move.

"You feel amazing, Baby. I'm okay. Move. Oh God, please move."

I wanted him to move more than anything in this world right now. It seemed like Zane was on the same page as me, because he was instantly slowly pulling out before he pushed back in. He kept his pace slow and smooth. It should have driven me insane, but surprisingly enough it didn't. We hadn't had sex like this before, slow and sensual, it brought a whole new level of pleasure to me. Zane reached over and grabbed a pillow before he lifted my hips and slid it under them. The new position of my hips caused Zane to hit my sweet spot dead on each time.

"Zane!" I called out as pleasure shot straight up my spine, my balls pulling up tight to my body.

"That's it, Babe, let it out. I want the world to know that you are mine," Zane said as he kissed all along my neck before he sucked on it, giving me a hickey.

After our attack, I thought Zane would try and hide that fact that he was gay and in a relationship with me. But the opposite happened. He was all too happy to hold my hand and introduce himself as my boyfriend. It was like this wall had been blown up and Zane was now free to just be himself, and he loved it.

I loved it, too.

I was a sucker for a hickey. To have a mark that told people I belonged to someone.

Zane continued to hit my sweet spot and each time it made me see stars. I was so close. I just needed a little more. I moved my hand down to start touching myself, but it was quickly snatched up by Zane's hand. He moved my hands above my head and he took them into his own, keeping them there.

"Zane, please, faster. I'm so close."

"Not this time. Just close your eyes

and feel it. Let it build and then when you explode it's going to feel so fucking good." Zane's breath against my ear caused me to shiver and I slid my eyes closed, marveling at the pleasure just his words brought to me.

I had rarely come before without my cock being touched, but Zane seemed determined to make that happen and I was more than happy to lay here and be pleasured.

Zane's lips were back on mine, but his grip remained firm on my hands. I don't know what it was, perhaps a combination of everything, but my body was tingling from this position. I wasn't able to move my hands and touch him, but being held down, even just gently like this, sent an extra wave of pleasure throughout my body. It was something we would need to play around with later.

I could feel Zane getting closer. His dick was getting harder, swelling inside of me and I was right there with him. I was so close. That moment finally came when Zane hit my sweet spot once more with a hard thrust and I exploded.

"Zane!" I screamed out as my back arched and I felt my dick pulsing hard and long. I couldn't stop moaning as my cock throbbed and the cum continued to pulse out of me, covering my belly and chest with slippery white ropes. I had never come this hard or long before, it was like it was never going to stop. My whole body was trembling from the pure pleasure that this single orgasm had brought to me.

The tightening of my walls was enough to push Zane over the edge. He screamed my name as his hot cum shot inside of me. The heat from it and the sensation of feeling him pulse only caused me to come more. I had no idea it would feel like this. The heat alone was enough to drive me mad, but to feel it in combination with his dick throbbing within me, I was in heaven.

Condoms between us definitely needed to stop.

I could never go back to using them after this.

I opened my eyes and saw Zane staring back at me. The arousal was clear in his eyes, but so was something else. A deep passion, a connection that we now shared with the other. It was sacred and something that would always remain special between us.

He leaned forward and began a

session of slow and sweet kisses. He removed his hands from mine, allowing me to run them through his hair as our bodies started to come down from the intense high we just felt.

When the need for air became too much for the both of us, Zane pulled back, but only slightly. He cupped my cheek with his hand before he said the words I had been longing to hear.

"I love you."

My heart actually fluttered.

I thought that was just something they wrote in books or in the movies, but it actually happened. Hearing those three simple words coming out of Zane was a dream come true. I knew I had fallen in love with him a few months ago, but I never wanted to say it. Too afraid that it would scare him off and I would be left alone and heartbroken. He was taking a huge risk by telling me, but it was going to be a risk that paid off very well.

"I love you, too," I said with as much love in my voice as I could muster.

The warmth and joy that filled his eyes told me everything I ever needed to know. His love was true and deep within him and to know that I loved him back was all he needed to hear.

I pulled Zane in for a kiss, one that quickly went from slow and sweet to hard and heated. I could feel Zane's dick getting hard once again inside of me and I knew that our afternoon was just starting.

***

Lying here in Zane's arms made

everything feel perfect. Since the attack, things between us had been different. He was different. I couldn't hold it against him, though. After all, he was the one that remembered. I didn't have those memories, something I still felt blessed about. I didn't want those memories. I didn't need those memories to haunt me for the rest of my life.

What hurt me was knowing that Zane did have the memories. He remembered everything from that night and I hated that for him. I knew it would take time for him to recover from the mental scars the attack had left him with. I completely understood that, but that didn't mean it wasn't hard.

When he had been pulling away from me, afraid to touch me for the past month, something felt like it cut very deep inside of me. I wanted to be intimate with the man I loved. I wanted to be held and kissed by him and, damn it, I wanted to have sex with him. I wanted to know that he still wanted me that way. That he was here with me because he wanted me and not out of some obligation built on false guilt from what happened that night in the park. The attack aside, he'd acted like he was avoiding me, and that cut deep after all we'd meant to each other. It scared me.

So, to feel his hands on me again, to see that desire in his eyes, it completely obliterated my worst fears. Zane did in fact still want me, he still found me attractive. Our relationship was still intact and that eased all of my worries and fears. I felt the most immense relief once all that uncertainty had been laid to rest.

The sound of Zane's phone dinging made him pull away. I knew he had been texting with his little brother a lot in the past month and Zane was making a real habit of being there for him. Whenever Daryl texted, Zane always made sure he responded. He would call him to check in and see how school was going at least once a week, too.

I knew he was worried about him and I couldn't blame him. Zane had said his parents were different, that his father was strict and had very traditional beliefs. Part of me, though, foolishly believed that his parents would be okay with him being gay, as long as he was happy. It was a stupid idea considering how Danny's parents had reacted to him coming out. I mean, I'd seen it before so

I should have known it could easily be the case with Zane's parents. Maybe it was me just being hopeful for Zane that things with his parents wouldn't be as bad. Boy, was I wrong.

Still, though, Zane admitted it in a hospital after getting attacked. He was injured and in pain.

How could any parent just walk away from their child when they were like that?

I knew it was bothering him, even if he didn't want to show it or say it. Him getting that letter from their family lawyer telling him he was no longer getting his inheritance, it cut him deep. It wasn't just about his dream of opening a resort, it was the act of his parents trying to erase him from their lives.

To begin with, that money was money

he earned. Money that was left to him by previously deceased family members, it wasn't like his parents put the money into the account. It was from generations as it was passed down through the family. That was his rightful money and they had no right to try and take that from him.

I told him I felt he should fight it, that he shouldn't let his parents away with it, but he was so worried about what that could mean for Daryl. He didn't want to rock the boat and potentially put his brother in a worse position. I could understand that, respect it, but it was still hard seeing him struggle with this.

I reached over and opened the bedside table drawer and pulled out my sketchbook and pencils. After moving my pillows up, I sat back and started to sketch the man that I loved lying in my bed. He always looked so sexy after sex. The way his hair was slightly messy from my fingers, this peaceful look on his face, as if all of the pieces that make him up were perfectly in place. There was no outside stress, no pressure or expectations from his family or so-called friends. He was just Zane and he was breathtaking.

"How is Daryl?" I asked, after he placed his phone down. He didn't move, though, knowing that I was sketching him. I had told him in the early days of our relationship that I wanted to sketch him, that he was the perfect model. Today, after six months, I was finally getting my wish.

"I think he's lying to me," Zane said, clearly feeling completely troubled.

"About what?"

"About how bad it's getting."

"What makes you think that? I thought he'd been open and honest with you about what has been going on this past month."

I knew things were a bit rocky at the house for Daryl. It was natural that after his parents discovered that Zane was gay it would change the dynamic at the house. All of that disappointment and anger had to go somewhere and with Zane not there, it was logical for Daryl to be the target of those emotions. It wasn't fair, but with Zane not there, it would naturally progress down to Daryl.

"He was in the beginning. He was telling me everything that was going on. Now, though, his answers are getting shorter, he's taking longer to answer my texts, and he's avoiding my calls. It seems like he's trying to hide things from me," Zane said with a great deal of worry to his voice.

"Maybe he's been busy. He's seventeen and in high school. School is over in three months so he might have a lot of projects going on right now," I said, trying to find a more positive reason as to why Daryl's texts were getting shorter and further apart.

"After the attack, he said Father was constantly yelling and throwing things. Trying to figure out who to blame for my *disease*. Going on and on about faggots and how he was worried about Daryl catching it. He destroyed my room, everything that Daryl wasn't able to pack up for me. He was ranting and raving about how he was going to have to cover it all up now, try to explain why me and Kayla weren't going to work. How me being a disgusting fag was going to destroy this big deal."

I could hear the hurt within his voice. He was trying to hide it, trying to put up a front that his own father's words didn't bother him, but they did. I hated that he felt like he needed to be strong right now. That he needed to always be strong.

He had been working a lot of hours at the diner to try and make enough money to get a two bedroom apartment for him and Daryl. Daryl couldn't move until he was eighteen, eight months from now, but Zane wanted to be ready for when he was able to legally move.

What I wasn't sure about was why he was so worried about Daryl. I knew he liked to draw and was creative, but Zane seemed very worried about how Daryl would be at the house. He didn't like that he was there alone, but I couldn't help but wonder if there was more to it.

"There isn't anything wrong with you. You don't have a *disease*. We were born this way. Just like he was born straight. You can't take his words personally, Baby. Is there something going on with Daryl? Something that you haven't told me?" I asked gently. I didn't want to make it sound like an accusation or that I thought there was something wrong with Daryl. That wasn't it at all. I didn't really know Daryl, I had yet to meet him. All I knew about him was what Zane had shared, which wasn't much really.

"I forgot I never told you. Daryl, he's gay," Zane stated.

Holy shit.

That explained a lot.

It explained everything that Zane was going through. Why he was so worried about him, why he was working all of these hours to save up enough for a two bedroom apartment. He didn't want Daryl to have to go through what he did. To feel like he had to hide a huge part of who he was. It wasn't an easy life for someone to go through and not one anyone would wish upon another, especially someone you love.

"I'm sorry. I'm not sorry that he's gay," I quickly clarified. "I'm sorry he's having to go through the explosion of negativity and nastiness that is your father. I hope he knows that whatever garbage your father says, it's not a reflection of him. Neither of you have a *disease.* There isn't anything wrong with you or him. Unfortunately, some people don't understand and their mind is too closed off to see what is right in front of them."

"I don't know how he feels about what is being said. He doesn't talk about it. He'll tell me about it, but he doesn't tell me what he's feeling. I'm worried he's bottling it all up, pushing it down. He used to paint, but now Father has gone through the entire house and taken everything away that he could use for a creative outlet. He said only fags draw and paint. He's pushing Daryl into more *manly* activities. Before this, Daryl seemed to be pretty comfortable with who he is. He seemed to be in a better place with his sexuality than I was at his age. But anything could change if you hear enough poison being yelled all day long." Zane sighed.

"It can be, but you also have to remember he has you. He sees you and your life and he knows that you aren't some horrible person. It sounds like he's more at peace with who he is than you were at that age. That's a really good sign. He just needs to make it eight more months and then he can leave and live with you."

"If I can get him through these next eight months," Zane said.

The first stage of doubt was starting to creep in and I could tell he was seriously starting to worry if he could get his brother through these next eight months.

"We will get him through this. Together," I said with as much strength to my voice that I could. Zane needed to know that I was in his corner and I was also in Daryl's corner. They didn't have to go through this alone. I would be there to support them in any way that I could.

Zane gave me a warm smile as he reached up and pulled me in for a kiss. Even after all this time, the feeling of his lips against mine still sent shivers down my spine. The connection I felt with Zane was the most intense connection I had ever had. I couldn't imagine what my life would be like without him in it. I didn't want to. He pulled back after a moment when the need for air became too much for the both of us.

"I love you."

Butterflies filled my stomach at hearing those sweet words again from his lips. I was never going to get tired of hearing them.

"I love you, too," I easily said back. "Now, stay still. I'm trying to create my best masterpiece yet."

Zane's rich laugh filled my chest with a deep warmth. It was good to hear him laugh. I hadn't heard it since before the attack. It was music to my ears.

"Should I remove the blanket?" Zane said with a playful wink.

"Hell no. The only one that gets to know what your dick looks like is me. That massive friend of yours is only for my eyes and pleasure." And oh was there ever pleasure with this man.

"The only body my friend wants is your body. You never have to worry about that, Babe."

"I know. Have you had any luck with

finding an apartment?"

The real estate world in town wasn't that great. It wasn't often people were moving, so it could be a bit of work finding an apartment, especially a two bedroom. Thankfully, my parents were amazing people and had no problem with Zane staying here.

"Not yet. I'm just working as much as I can and saving up so I will be ready when one comes available. I'm not real picky about where it is or what it looks like."

"What are you going to do about the resort? I know you don't have your inheritance anymore, but you shouldn't let that stop you from pursuing your dreams."

I didn't want Zane feeling like he needed to settle, now. He had a dream.

Something I believed could really work for the town. It was something he was passionate about. He shouldn't be giving that up. Yes, not having his inheritance was a roadblock but it was one he could get around. I truly believed that.

"I'm not giving up. I'm focusing on completing my business course right now. Then I'll get a business plan put together and start looking for investors. I'm not letting anyone stop me from building it. My Father doesn't get to win," Zane said with a deep determination to his voice.

It made me very proud and happy to hear that Zane was still going to pursue his dreams of opening a resort. I had no idea how it would all work, I wasn't a business person at all, but I was willing to help him with whatever he needed and I would always be a sounding board to him. No matter what was going to happen in the future, we would face it together.

EPILOGUE

Zane

I COULDN'T BELIEVE it had been eight months since I first kissed Jimmy. These past eight months had been a roller coaster ride, to say the least, but it was a roller coaster I never wanted to get off. If you had told me that working as a manager in a diner would lead me to finding my soul mate, I would have thought you were insane.

Yet, that is exactly what happened.

The best decision I had ever made in my life was applying for that job. It led me to Jimmy and I wouldn't trade him for anything in the world. Even though I had lost my parents, I had gained so much more. I had Jimmy and his amazing parents on my side.

His parents were truly wonderful human beings and I am a better person, a better man, for having them in my life. The loss of my parents was hard. Even though we didn't get along, we didn't see the world the same way, they were still my parents. I still wanted to have their approval, their love. Having to accept that it wasn't something that was going to happen was hard, maybe harder than it should have been. It wasn't like I didn't know it would happen, eventually. I guess I just had myself believing that in five years they might have felt differently.

I was coming to peace with it, having Jimmy and his family in my life had definitely helped me come to peace with it all. Now that I was out and proud, I was finding that, internally, I wasn't so torn up. I felt complete, like the weight that had been on my shoulders was finally removed. I had no idea that something like coming out would make me feel this good. Finally, I was able to be myself completely without having to hide pieces of myself or live a double life. I could focus on the future.

My future with Jimmy.

Today was a very big day for him. Today he was finally graduating high school and what made it sweeter, was that he would be able to walk across the stage without crutches or a cane.

The past two months had been hard on him with his physical therapy, but Jimmy never gave up. He pushed through all of the pain and did every single exercise that he was told to do. He worked his ass off just for this single moment. Just so he could walk across the stage for his diploma without needing any help. It was the one main driving force pushing Jimmy through all of the pain and endless hours exercising. He wanted to be able to graduate high school as he had always envisioned he would. He wanted to graduate and put the attack completely behind him and have his future clear in front of him. All of his hard work was paying off and I couldn't have been more proud of him.

SHATTERED

"I'm so nervous for him," Jimmy's mother said beside me.

We were all sitting in the third row, the closest we could get as the first two rows were reserved for the graduating class. We had gotten here an hour early just so we could get a good seat in the front. Both of his parents had been balls of nervous and excited energy. We all had our phones ready and they were constantly checking the battery life on theirs, even though they had charged them all night and before we left the house.

I could understand why they were excited. It wasn't just the fact that their only child was graduating high school with honors, but he was going to be walking without his cane.

Jimmy had been able to complete his

last physical therapy session a week ago and he had been walking without his cane for the past three days. His leg was doing a lot better, but it was still healing so he had to be careful for the next few weeks to not aggravate his injury.

"He's going to do great," I said, flashing his mother an encouraging smile.

Jimmy had worked hard on not just his physical therapy, but with his schooling. He had been out of school with his leg injuries and physical therapy for a good six weeks before he could go back. He had been working from home on his schoolwork so he wouldn't get behind and potentially lose the semester, making him unable to graduate.

Not graduating was not an option for

Jimmy. For any of us. He had a full ride scholarship waiting for him, there was no way in hell any of us were going to allow what those assholes did to him to cost him his future. He was going to school in the fall and he would be doing it without a limp or any lingering pain.

"How is your apartment?" Jimmy's father asked.

I had stayed with them for two months, something I would always be grateful for, before a two bedroom finally became available. I jumped on it right away. Especially because it was in a good location. It wasn't far from work, so I could walk and save money on gas without having to drive. It also wasn't too far from Jimmy's house, which made it easier for us to see each other more.

Now, I was just working on saving up

some money so I could afford to buy a bed for Daryl and some things for his bedroom so he would be all set to move in when he turned eighteen in six months. Having my own place for the first time in my life, though, felt amazing. I could just be myself and not have to worry about always having to be on guard. At Jimmy's, I could relax as well, but there is something different about living on your own. I have every intention of enjoying it while I can before Daryl moves in.

"It's great. I have everything set up and now I'm just getting used to being on my own and making sure I actually have food that I'm cooking." I chuckled.

Cooking was an interesting experience for me. Most people at my age have cooked or have the knowledge and skills to make simple things. However, we had always had someone else cooking for us, even breakfast. My father refused to cook and my mother held zero interest in it, so a cook was what we grew up with. Now, I had to figure it all out for myself.

Thankfully, YouTube was a huge asset that I had right at my fingertips. There had been plenty of days where I'd cooked along with whoever was on my screen. I was getting somewhere and, it turns out I actually enjoyed cooking. It made the food taste better somehow to know I'd actually created it myself. And then there was that sense of accomplishment, too.

"Well, you just remember that if you ever need a cooking lesson, I am available. I love to cook and bake,"

Jimmy's mother said with that warm smile of hers.

"I would love to learn how to bake, but I think I'm going to stick with cooking for now. Maybe once I have more dishes under my belt, I'll start to figure out baking." I flashed her a grin.

The idea of baking did appeal to me, but I needed to make sure I didn't burn down my new apartment before I attempted to bake anything. Not burning the eggs was a new accomplishment recently. It was a slow growth, but I was getting there.

Music started to play and we all sat up in our seats as the ceremony started. I could see and feel the energy in the auditorium. Everyone was excited for the graduating class, including the class themselves. Most of them could barely sit still.

I easily remembered when I graduated high school. Most of the people in my graduating class were all excited to be getting the summer off to relax and travel before they went off to their colleges. I just remember feeling like I was stuck in quicksand, unable to move, otherwise I would sink to the bottom and die. I didn't get to go and travel for two months. I didn't get to apply for any colleges. My future had been dictated to me and there was nothing I could do about it.

This time, though, I could enjoy the energy and atmosphere within the auditorium. The excitement and anticipation of their whole lives laid out before them, it was something that I could relate to this time around. This time, I could share in their excitement. Because now, my whole life was mine to control and dictate. I was free and it was intoxicating.

"Jimmy Ashford," the presenter announced once they started giving out the diplomas.

We were instantly on our feet cheering and clapping. He looked amazing in his black cap and gown as he walked up the four steps and across the stage. You couldn't even tell that he had a leg injury. He walked strong and confident, with his head held up high. He was breathtaking and I couldn't wait until tonight when we could sneak away to my apartment.

Jimmy turned and gave us a brilliant smile and wave as he received his diploma, and then he had to make his way off stage and back to his seat. It took everything in me not to run over there and hug him, but I would have to wait until the ceremony was over. Then he would be mine.

I would need to remind myself that we were in public, so all I could do was hug and give him a simple kiss. Tonight, though, I would be showing him exactly how proud of him I am.

***

The backyard was packed back at Jimmy's house. He had his parents, his grandparents, and his friends here, including Danny and his older brother, Thad. I could see that Thad was exhausted. He clearly had been working a lot of hours and was feeling stressed.

I felt bad for him. They were going

through a lot and there was no telling just how bad the fight could be with their parents. I hoped they got some sense knocked into them soon and left Danny and Thad alone.

I couldn't help but look down at my phone again for the hundredth time. I had invited Daryl to the barbeque, but so far he hadn't shown. He said he would, but that was a week ago and I hadn't heard from him since. Our conversations were getting shorter and with more time in between. Even when I texted him, he would send me a response, normally one word, a week later. Something was going on at home and I was worried about what it could be.

"Hey, Baby, you okay?" Jimmy asked, flashing me a big smile, but there was a hint of worry in his tone.

I put my phone away and forced my mind to focus on what was going on around me. I would simply have to keep reaching out to Daryl and make sure he knew that I was at least there for him for whenever he was ready.

"Yes, I'm good. Have I told you how sexy you are today?"

Jimmy currently wore dark blue skinny jeans that were one of three pairs of pants that didn't have paint on them. He'd paired them with his paint splattered converse shoes and a red t-shirt. He looked very sexy tonight.

"You may have mentioned it a few times. I have been told we can't sneak away until after the cake."

"Oh, you've been told? Did we get found out?" I asked, flashing him a grin.

"My mom figured it out. She even gave me a wink to go with it," Jimmy said with a small chuckle. His parents were amazing, they seriously were.

The smile on my face instantly disappeared when I saw my brother walking into the backyard. Him being here wasn't what took my smile away. It was the very clear black eye on his face.

My anger mounted and I could feel the heat infuse my face. Jimmy glanced over his shoulder to see what I was looking at and when he saw Daryl, his face paled.

"I'm just going to go over here," Jimmy said, putting a reassuring hand on my shoulder and acknowledging that he knew I would need a minute alone with my brother. Just another reason why I loved that man.

Daryl made his way toward me and I could see he was feeling defensive already without me even saying anything. I had no idea what happened to him, though I had a few guesses. I was going to find out.

"I'm fine," Daryl instantly said before I could even open my mouth.

"Who did it?" I demanded with an edge to my voice. I swear to god, if our father laid a hand on him, I was going to kill him. Jail or no jail.

"Just some guy, it's not a big deal. I'm fine," Daryl said, but he couldn't make eye contact with me. He sucked at lying to me. He could lie to anyone, but he couldn't do it with me for some reason. He had been like that since he was a little boy.

"Bullshit. Did Father do that to you?"

"No, I'm fine, okay? You don't have to worry about me. I'll be eighteen in six months and then, legally, I'll be an adult and can do whatever I want."

He put up a brave front, for sure. I could see through it, though. He was worried, he was uncertain, and he was scared.

Six months might not sound all that long, but it was forever when you were in a place that wasn't safe. A place that could hurt you physically, but also emotionally and mentally.

I hated knowing I had to leave him there. If my parents weren't rich, it would have been easy to have Daryl just stay with me. They wouldn't have an image they needed to upkeep. But they did have an image, and my father would kill to protect it. Me trying to take Daryl from them, it would only make his home situation worse. That didn't mean I couldn't still be there for him, though. And I would, no matter what.

I reached into my pocket and pulled out my spare key that I was going to give Jimmy tonight. I handed it to Daryl as I spoke.

"This is your key to my apartment. If you need to get away, just say you are staying at a friend's place. I have a two bedroom and I'm working on getting a bed for you, but one of us can always crash on the couch. I want you safe, that's all that matters."

Daryl looked at the key for a moment before he finally took it and pocketed it. "Thanks, but I'm fine. Really, Z."

No, he wasn't, but he clearly needed the break from the drama and stress today. I would have to talk to him more about what was going on at home later, but giving him some peace now, that was something I could do for him.

"There's still some food, why don't you grab something to eat and relax," I suggested, giving him a warm smile.

The relief was evident on his face as he gave me a nod and headed off.

I watched as he made his way over to the food table. I was hoping he would mingle with some of Jimmy's friends and maybe make some that wouldn't care he was gay.

The second I was alone, Jimmy instantly came back over to me.

"He okay?" he asked, his voice laced with a deep concern for my brother.

"He's lying about where it came from. I think our father did it, but he won't admit to it. Just keeps saying he's fine. I gave him the key that I actually made for you to my apartment," I said with a shy smile. That was technically his graduation gift.

"He needs it a lot more than I do, Baby. We can always make another one. They are easy to replace. But it gives him something irreplaceable, a safe place he knows he can go to if he needs it," Jimmy said with a deep understanding.

"I'll have to talk to him more about it, but I don't want to push him tonight. He looks like he could use the break from our family. He needs a few hours to just be a seventeen year old kid."

"He's not the only one that needs to relax and have some fun," Jimmy said as he put his arm through mine. "Come on, let's mingle and have some fun."

I couldn't deny him that. This was his day and I wanted to make sure he had a great time. He was so special and we both had our whole lives ahead of us. I had no idea what the future would hold for either of us. But what I did know, with the utmost certainty, was that my future would involve this amazing, kind, creative and brave young man.

Both of our futures looked bright, now, and I couldn't wait to see what life had in store for us.

Thank you for reading!

Watch for Runaway, From The Edge,
Book Two, at your favorite online
retailer.

Turn the page for a preview!

PREVIEW

Daryl

THE WARM SUN against my skin felt better than it ever had before. It sounds crazy, but feeling the sun against your skin after finally becoming free, there's just something exciting in it, exhilarating even.

Free.

It sounds like I was in prison or

locked away in some dark and damp cellar by a serial killer. The truth is, I was just outside yesterday and every day before that. I've never been in prison. I've never been trapped in a small room and told what I could do, what I could eat. There was no serial killer causing me harm. I had every freedom that a normal human being has, and yet, I felt as if I *was* trapped. Not physically, but mentally and emotionally.

It had been almost a year since my older brother, Zane, came out to our parents. It wasn't planned; more of a heat of the moment type of deal when he was in the hospital after him and his boyfriend, Jimmy, were attacked. They still hadn't found who had committed the brutal assault, and chances were they were never going to. They had both made peace with it, something I don't think I could have done. They were happy, though.

Zane had gotten a two bedroom apartment and Jimmy went off to College. He stays with Zane on weekends and on breaks. Currently, Jimmy was back for his four month summer vacation and, from what I have been told, they are inseparable when they aren't working.

I was proud of Zane. He was my big brother and I looked up to him a lot growing up. We have almost four years between us and when we were younger it was great. He was always teaching me something.

That four year difference, though, started to matter once he was thirteen and he didn't want to have his nine year old kid brother hanging around. We drifted apart for a while, a long while, really. It wasn't until he started working at the diner did we start to reconnect. I hadn't realized how much I had missed him until that day in our backyard.

When he came out, a flood of emotions hit me. I was slightly annoyed, because I had come out to him just months prior and he never said he was gay, too. That would have been the perfect opportunity for him to share something very personal with me.

Especially the fact that he was gay.

I was also very proud, though, because I knew what he gave up. I had made peace with the fact that I would lose my family, lose my inheritance. I was prepared for it and, to me, it wasn't worth more stress and having to deny who I was at my core.

Zane, though, he had plans. He had big plans for that money and he wasn't willing to go against our father if that meant he would lose his inheritance. When he threw it all away for love, I couldn't have been more proud of him. He made a huge sacrifice, one I knew I would be making soon enough. That sacrifice, though, became a lot less terrifying knowing I would have him in my corner.

The past ten months hasn't been easy. The exact opposite. My mother had always been indifferent with us, but now she was completely checked out. Most days, she didn't even say a word to me. It was like a zombie had taken over her body and she was just going through the motions. As for my father, well he got worse.

Before the incident, as we'll call it, he was tolerable. He wasn't loving and he had never been the type of father that checked under your bed for monsters. There were no hugs; no I love yous. He was just there and you knew not to cross him. He cared about the image of his company above all else and we all knew that we had to live up to his expectations.

When you are young and innocent that is very easy to do. However, when you start to grow up and hit the teenage years, it's natural that you would want to rebel and come into your own.

We didn't do that.

The fear had already been instilled into us, even though he never raised a hand to us. My father had this unique ability to destroy you with just a few words and we knew by a single look just how much trouble we were potentially walking into.

I was twelve when I discovered that I had zero interest in girls. Changing for gym class was always hard for me. I had to make sure I kept my eyes down and didn't look at anyone for fear that my body would react. It turned out, I wasn't the only one who had that issue. Billy Swanson was fighting his own feelings of confusion and attraction.

I was thirteen when we had discovered that the other was gay as well. We had decided to create a pact with each other. A safe zone, if you will. We would get to explore our sexuality, but with each other. We shared our first kiss, first handjob, and even first blowjob before Billy started to date a guy from another school and I was left without my safe zone.

That was, until I was sixteen and discovered Brad, my recent ex. He was deep in the closet like I was, so it seemed perfect. We had hit it off right away and within a week we were having sex.

I guess I'd always moved fast when it came to boyfriends. I don't really see the point in waiting for the right time or some special time to make a move. If I'm attracted to someone and they feel the same, then why wait? Life was short and I had zero interest in wasting any of my time on this Earth.

Brad and me didn't work out. He went and cheated on me, with a girl no less. Since then, I've kept to myself, trying to hide out from the hurricane that was my father. With the bomb that his oldest son, the one that was supposed to take over the company and bring it to a whole new level with marrying Kayla, was gay, he got worse.

I had no idea my father could yell so loudly and that much. He was constantly breaking things, throwing things, ranting and raving about how Zane had this *disease* and we couldn't let it infect me.

I knew I had to get out of there. I just needed to bide my time until I could graduate high school and be on my own.

Zane already had a place for me. He knew one day I would be living with him. All I needed to do was say the word.

I've been working my ass off these past ten months to graduate early. I was now eighteen and, as of yesterday, a high school graduate. I had four months off before I would be heading for College in Baltimore.

The past ten months hadn't been easy.

Zane and me were texting and calling each other, but it'd been getting further and further apart. That wasn't on him, it was completely on me.

I've been distancing myself from him to save him from the stress and drama of the house. He had enough on his plate, he didn't need to worry about me to go with it.

My father's words hurt, but I knew I couldn't take them personally. It was hard, because he was my father and I expected that he would love me regardless, but that just wasn't the case.

Zane had suspected it, but I'd never

confirmed that our father had been hitting me. I've stopped counting how many bruises he had put on my body.

There wasn't one thing over another that would trigger my father to lash out at me. Sometimes I would wear something that he felt was gay clothing. Sometimes it was just talking about a male friend. Sometimes it was when I was painting.

Straight men aren't artistic in my father's eyes.

It was always when he could justify my appearance or actions as that of someone *infected*. Apparently, his cure was beating it out of me. It's why I worked my ass off to graduate early. The sooner I could get out of that house, the better.

Today was that day.

I was free.

I had no home, barely any money, and no job, but I did have my car and I had Zane. Most importantly, I had my freedom. Everything else could be worked out.

I walked into the diner where I knew my brother would currently be working. I wasn't sure if Jimmy was on shift or not, but I didn't see him in the dining room. There were a few customers, but they didn't pay me any attention.

I headed behind the counter, past the kitchen, and into the back office. I knew technically I wasn't supposed to be back here, but it wasn't the first time.

I easily found Zane in the office filling out paperwork. He looked up at the sound of the door closing and I could instantly see the surprise and anger that flashed across his face.

I was expecting both.

The bruising from my most recent beating and the resulting black eye was still visible. It wasn't as dark as it had been a few days ago, but it was still noticeable.

"For fuck's sake, I'm going to kill him," Zane said with a deadly edge to his voice.

"Don't bother, he's not worth it." It was the first time I had admitted that the bruises had come from our father. I didn't feel one way or the other about it. It just kinda became a small piece of my history and I was determined to not let it affect me. I wasn't going to let him have power over me. "I graduated yesterday."

"What? No, your graduation is in June," Zane said, furrowing his brows, clearly confused by what I was talking about.

"The ceremony is, but I took extra courses so I could graduate early. Officially, I'm a high school graduate as of yesterday. I packed my bag this morning, went down to have breakfast, where I told Father that I love sucking dick, and then I left. I heard the table flip over as I was shutting the door."

It was a risk telling my father that I was gay, but even if I had it to do over, it was one I would always take. I wanted him to know the reason why I was leaving. I wanted him to know that not one, but both of his sons were gay and there was nothing he could do about it. That I wasn't going to hide. I was going to make sure this whole town knew I was gay. He wasn't going to disown me and pretend that I was dead. He was going to have to deal with my face around town.

"Good for you. I'm so proud of you," Zane said, flashing me a big warm smile as he got up and pulled me in for a hug.

I easily hugged him back. I had missed how his hugs felt. He had a way of making me always feel loved and safe. After a moment, he pulled back and I spoke.

"I hope I still have that room at your place."

"It's our place and always. I have two rules, though, but they are simple and easy to follow."

"Okay," I said, slightly unsure. I wasn't really certain what type of rules Zane would have for me. Truth be told, I was hoping to live rule free.

"You go to College and get yourself a degree so you are not working in a dead end job for the rest of your life. And you need to get a part-time job to help cover your expenses. I can cover the rent, but you need to pitch in for food and to cover your car expenses."

"So, be an adult. That I can do," I said with a warm smile. I'd already planned to look for a job to help out with bills and cover my own needs. I wasn't expecting him to do that.

"Perfect. Jimmy is at his parents for dinner so he will be home late. I'll text him and let him know you'll be there. You have a key already and your room is all set up. Let me know if you need any help with College applications or figuring out a program to take."

"I've already been accepted to the

University of Baltimore for the computer programming degree. I'm going to learn how to build video games. I even got a scholarship from my gaming app that I designed." I flashed him a brilliant smile, the first true smile I'd been able to let out in a very long time. I was proud of all I had accomplished, despite my father and his abuse.

I had a love of painting and drawing, but what people didn't realize was what I was doing with it. I would draw characters for video game ideas that I had floating around in my head. The work was peaceful and it allowed me to see what the characters were supposed to look like.

"I had no idea you designed a video game app. Why didn't you tell me?" Zane looked surprised, his eyebrows arched.

"I didn't think you would really care. We didn't really have the best relationship for a few years there. I just kept it to myself," I said, and shrugged.

I wasn't too sure how people would react to discovering that I was really into video games and developing them. Most teenage boys like playing video games, but to me it wasn't a hobby or a pastime. I was in love with them. I would always try to find glitches in their programming, constantly look for hidden programming in the game. They were my passion and I wanted to grow my skills and spend the rest of my life creating pieces of art.

"I know I was distant with you and I'm sorry for that. I want to know *you,* though. I want to know these things. I think it's amazing that you love playing video games and have found a way to take that love and passion and turn it into a career. That's really great, Squirt," Zane said with a warm and proud smile that reached his eyes.

I hated that nickname, but apparently it wasn't going to go away. Oh well, could be worse. Right now I was simply happy that Zane appeared to be proud of me. That *someone* was, finally.

"I'll start looking for a job tomorrow and then I'll probably stay on campus during the week and be home on weekends."

"Yeah, that's what Jimmy does. It's not much of a drive, but it is if you are doing it twice a day. He's looking to rent a room in someone's house next year, you guys might be able to find something together."

"Yeah, I wouldn't mind that. He doing

okay?"

"He's doing great," Zane said proudly, and puffed out his chest. His love for the younger man shone in his eyes whenever he talked about him, and it was very clear Zane was proud of Jimmy, too.

Jimmy had gone through a lot from the attack, including physical therapy. He never got his memories back, but I think they were taking that as a blessing.

It had taken time, but Zane seemed to have recovered from it. They had gone through something horrific together and they came out stronger than ever in the end. I couldn't have been more proud of either of them.

"That's good. All right, I'll get out of your hair. I have to unpack and start looking for work. I'll see you tonight."

"Yes, you will, at home," Zane said, and flashed me a wink and a grin.

I couldn't help the chuckle that slipped from my lips. It sounded so weird that I was going to be living with my brother, in our own apartment. I never expected for this to ever happen, but I was looking forward to spending more time with him.

We weren't kids anymore.

We could have a real relationship, not only between brothers, but friends, too. I was really looking forward to that.

Zane and Jimmy were the only family I had left, now. We were a small family, but that never mattered to me. We all had each other and Jimmy's parents, who are amazing people.

Together, we would grow our own family and there was nothing that could stop us.

***

I arrived at the apartment and a flood of emotions hit me the second I walked through the door.

The first was disappointment.

Frustration in myself because I hadn't been here before.

Zane had been the one to put some distance between us growing up, but it was me that placed that wall there this time around. I had been focusing all of my energy on making it through each day, so much so that I couldn't allow myself to get close to Zane. I couldn't afford the disappointment if something were to go wrong. It was just easier to not come by whenever I was invited. Seeing the apartment for the first time shouldn't have been now and that was all on me.

I was also hit with excitement.

Anticipation of what was to come.

I had my whole future now free to do whatever I wanted with it. I was very happy about it.

The last emotion was a shockwave of anxiety that took over my body from my toes all the way up to my head. It was gone within moments, but the fact that it was there to begin with told me I hadn't exactly walked away from my father's abuse as cleanly as I thought I did.

The anxiety of him finding out where I lived, of trying to get me back, was something I would need to deal with. I had no idea if he would let me go as easily as he had Zane. I was his youngest, but also his last child that could take over the family empire.

He cared about his image and that meant if he couldn't leave his family empire to one of his sons, an empire that had been in the family for many generations, it would leave a black stain on his image. The only way to prevent that would be for him to leave it to one of his *gay* sons.

My father would never be able to leave it to a gay man, which meant he would have to try and convince one of us to go back into the closet. Considering Zane and Jimmy were not shy about kissing in public, the only one that could go back into the closet was me. I wasn't about to let that happen, but it meant I would be hearing from my father eventually and my gut was telling me it would likely be sooner rather than later.

Pushing that thought aside, I made my way through the apartment to check it all out. My room was a decent size and there was a bathroom separating mine and Zane's bedrooms. I had a feeling I was going to appreciate the added sound barrier between us.

I placed my bag down on the bed and took a deep breath in and I let it out slowly. This was the start of my future and I wasn't going to let anyone ruin it, least of all my father.

Watch for Runaway at your favorite online retailer.

If you enjoyed Shattered, the first book in the From The Edge series, please return to your retailer and leave a review. Even a few words can mean the world to an author. Plus it helps other readers like you find our work too. Share the love! ;)

OTHER BOOKS BY EVIE

Federal Protection Agency
Mason
Rafe
Ryzen
Cooper
Noah
Damien
Sebastian
Gabe
Logan

Ruthless Empire
Courting Danger
Chasing Danger
Kissing Danger

Smokejumpers
Hawke
Cyrus
Jase
Gage
Jackson
Xavier

Jasper Springs
Cade
Dawson
Drew
Grayson
Riley
Mitch

From The Edge
Shattered
Runaway
Jaded
Rescue
Hidden
Tormented

Gray Vale Pack
His Fated Mate
His Wounded Warrior
His Healing Heart

ABOUT THE AUTHOR

Evie Riley is a prolific, neurodivergent author known for her captivating MM romance novels. She has gained a significant following and topped the LGBT+ action and adventure bestseller charts with her series.

Evie's writing style often explores dark and gritty themes where her men must overcome difficult obstacles in their search for love, but she has also ventured into sweeter small-town romances, incorporating tropes like enemies-to-lovers, friends-to-lovers, age-gap, and forced proximity. She is known for crafting engaging romantic suspense novels and has a knack for creating interconnected series worlds that keep readers invested.

EVIE RILEY

Interestingly, Ms. Riley has hinted at exploring new genres, such as Alien Omegaverse Romance, in the future.

Outside of writing, she enjoys spending time at the beach and has a quirky personality, described by her partner as ranging from cute to deadly, depending on her blood-chocolate levels.

Evie spends her nights writing bad boys in love, and her days wrangling the sweet boys she loves.